This book belongs to

. . . .

. . . .

Lancashire County Library

30118131995353

FABER AND FABER has published children's books since 1929. Some of our very first publications included *Old Possum's Book of Practical Cats* by T. S. Eliot starring the now world-famous Mactivity, and *The Iron Man* by Ted Hughes. Our catalogue at the time said that 'it is by reading such books that children learn the difference between the shoddy and the genuine'. We still believe in the power of reading to trasform children's lives.

The Iron Woman

A Sequel to
The Iron Man

TED HUGHES was born in Yorkshire in 1930. His first book, *The Hawk in the Rain*, was published by Faber in 1957, and was followed by many volumes of poetry and prose for both children and adults. He was Poet Laureate from 1984 and was appointed to the Order of Merit in 1998, the year in which he died.

The Iron Woman

Ted Hughes

Illustrated by Andrew Davidson

FABER & FABER

First published in 1993 by Faber and Faber Limited
Bloomsbury House, 74–77 Great Russell Street
London WC1B 3DA
This edition first published in 2014

Designed and typeset by Crow Books

Printed and bound in Great Britain by
CPI Group (UK), Croydon CR0 4YY

All rights reserved
© The Estate of Ted Hughes, 1993
Illustrations © Andrew Davidson, 1993

Ted Hughes is hereby identified as the author of this work
in accordance with Section 77 of the Copyright, Designs and
Patents Act 1988

*This book is sold subject to the condition that it shall not,
by way of trade or otherwise, be lent, resold, hired out or
otherwise circulated without the publisher's prior consent in any
form of binding or cover other than that in which it is published and without
a similar condition including this condition being imposed
on the subsequent purchaser*

A CIP record for this book is available from the British Library

ISBN 978-0-571-31478-2

FSC
www.fsc.org
MIX
Paper from
responsible sources
FSC® C101712

2 4 6 8 10 9 7 5 3 1

For Frieda and Nicholas

Lancashire Library Services	
30118131995353	
PETERS	JF
£5.99	07-Dec-2015
EWH	

1

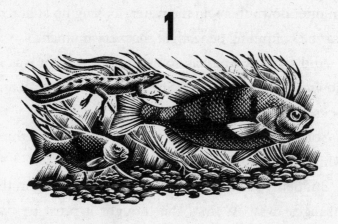

School was over and the Easter holidays had begun.
Lucy was walking home, between the reed banks,
along the marsh road, when it started to happen. She
had just come to the small bridge, where the road
goes over the deep drain. She called this Otterfeast
Bridge, because once she had seen an otter on the
edge of it, over the black water, eating an eel. That had
been three years before. But she still felt excitement
whenever she came to this part of the road, and she
always looked ahead eagerly, towards the bridge.

Today, as usual, the bridge was empty. As she crossed
over it, she looked between the rails, into the black

1

water. She always did this, just in case there might be an otter down there, in the water, looking up at her, or maybe swimming beneath at that very moment.

And today, there was something. But what was it, down there in the water? She leaned over the rail and peered.

Something deep in the dark water, something white, kept twisting. A fish?

Suddenly she knew. It was an eel – behaving in the strangest way. At first, she thought it must be two eels, fighting. But no, it was just one eel. It knotted itself and unknotted. Then it swam quickly round in circles, corkscrewing over and over as it went. At one point, its tail flipped right out of the water. Then it was writhing down into the mud, setting a grey cloud drifting. Then it was up at the surface again, bobbing its head into the air. She saw its beaky face, then its little mouth opening. She saw the pale inside of its mouth.

Then it was writhing and tumbling in a knot. Quite a small eel, only a foot long.

As it danced its squirming, circling, darting dance,

it was drifting along in the current of the drain. Soon she lost sight of it under the water shine. Then, twenty yards downstream, she saw its head bob up again. Then a swirl and it vanished. Then up again, bob, bob, bob.

What was wrong with it? Seeing its peculiar head bobbing up like that, and its little mouth opening, she had felt a painful twist somewhere in her middle. She had wanted to scoop the eel up and help it. It needed help. Something was wrong with it.

At that moment, staring along the dimpled shine of the drain where it curved away among the tall reeds, she felt something else.

At first, she had no idea what made her head go dizzy and her feet stagger. She gripped the bridge rail and braced her feet apart. She thought she had felt the rail itself give her hand a jolt.

What was it?

'Garronk! Garronk! Garraaaaaark!'

The floppy, untidy shape of a heron was scrambling straight up out of the reed beds. It did not flap away in stately slow motion, like an ordinary heron. It flailed

3

and hoisted itself up, exactly as if it were bounding up an invisible spiral stair. Then, from a great height, it tumbled away towards the sea beyond the marsh. Something had scared it badly. But what? Something in the marsh had frightened it. And seeing the heron so frightened frightened Lucy.

The marsh was always a lonely place. Now she felt the loneliness. As she stood there, looking up, the whole bluish and pinky sky of soft cloud moved slowly. She looked again along the drain, where the reeds leaned all one way, bowing gently in the light wind. The eel was no longer to be seen. Was it still writhing and bobbing its head up, as the slow flow carried it away through the marsh? She looked down into the drain, under the bridge. The black water moved silently, crumpling and twirling little whorls of light.

Then it came again. Beneath her feet the bridge road jumped and the rail jarred her hand. At the same moment, the water surface of the drain was blurred by a sudden mesh of tiny ripples all over it.

An earthquake! It must be an earthquake.

A completely new kind of fear gripped Lucy. For a few seconds she did not dare to move. The thought of the bridge collapsing and dropping her into the drain with its writhing eels was bad enough. But the thought of the marsh itself opening a great crack, and herself and all the water and mud and eels and reeds pouring into bottomless black, maybe right into the middle of the earth, was worse. She felt her toes curling like claws and the soles of her feet prickling with electricity.

Quickly then she began to walk – but it was like walking on a bouncy narrow plank between skyscrapers. She lifted each foot carefully and set it down firmly and yet gently. As fast as she dared, and yet quite slow. But soon – she couldn't help it – she started running. What if that earthquake shock had brought the ceiling down on her mother? Or even shaken the village flat, like dominoes? And what if some great towering piece of machinery, at the factory, had toppled on to her father?

And then, as she ran, it came again, pitching her off balance, so that her left foot hit her right calf and down she went. As she lay there, flat and winded, it came again. This time, the road seemed to hit her chest and stomach, a strong, hard thump. Then another. And each time, she saw the road gravel under her face jump slightly. And it was then, as she lay there, that she heard the weirdest sound. Nothing like any bird she had ever heard. It came from out of the marsh behind her. It was a long wailing cry, like a fire-engine siren. She jumped up and began to run blindly.

Already the head was out. It still didn't look much like a head – simply a gigantic black lump, crowned with reeds and streaming with mud. But the mouth was clear, and after that first wailing cry the lips moved slowly, like a crab's, spitting out mud and roots.

Half an hour passed before the lump moved again. As it moved, the reeds away to either side of it bulged upwards and heaved, and the black watery mud streamed through them. The mouth opened and a long booming groan came out of it, as the head hoisted clear. Another groan became a wailing roar. A seagull blowing across the marsh like a paper scrap veered wildly upwards as the streaming shape reared

6

in front of it, like a sudden wall of cliff, pouring cataracts of black mud and clotted, rooty lumps of reeds where grass snakes squirmed and water voles flailed their forepaws, blinking their eyes and squealing as they fell.

The black shape was the size of two or three elephants. It looked like a hippopotamus-headed, gigantic dinosaur, dragging itself on all fours up out of a prehistoric tar pit. But now, still like a dinosaur, it sat upright. And all at once it looked human – immense but human. Great hands clawed at the head, flinging away squatches of muddy reeds. Then, amid gurglings and suckings, and with a groaning wail, the thing stood erect. A truly colossal, man-shaped statue of black mud, raking itself and groaning, towered over the lonely marsh.

About half a mile away a birdwatcher was bent over a bittern's nest, holding a dead bittern and feeling the cold eggs on which the dead bird had been sitting. From his hide, only ten feet away, he had been watching this bird all day, waiting for the eggs to start hatching.

He knew the chicks were already overdue. When those first quakes had come, shuddering his camera on its tripod, he had told himself they were distant quarry blastings. He had guessed the strange wailing must be some kind of factory siren. He knew there was a big factory outside the town, only two or three miles away. What else could such things be? And when that second booming wail had come, he had just seen something far more startling. He stared through his binoculars. Two big blowflies were inspecting the eye of the bittern on the nest. With a shock, he realized the bird was dead. All day, and probably yesterday too, he had been watching a dead bird. This was more important than any noises. So he had waded out, and lifted the dead mother from her eggs. He was horrified. She was quite stiff.

And it was then, as he stood there, thinking that he must take this bird and her eggs to be examined by some scientist, to find out what had killed them, it was then that the third wail came, far louder than the earlier ones. At the same moment the marsh shook, like a vast jelly, and he thought: An earthquake!

8

And maybe that's a siren warning!

He had made his hide at the edge of some higher ground that stuck out into the marsh from the road. Big bushy willow trees behind him blocked his view of what had terrified the heron and the seagull. But he was alarmed enough by the idea of an earthquake. Cradling the cold eggs in one hand, with the dead bittern tucked under his arm, he collected his camera and returned to his car parked among the willows. As he opened the car door, another jolt shook it.

He drove out along grassy ruts on to the road, not far from the bridge where Lucy had stood watching the eel. As he turned right, towards the town, his eyes widened and his brain whirled. The swaying, lumpy, black tower, about a hundred yards ahead, close to the road, could not possibly be anything. Unless it was some structure for aerials, something to do with radar, maybe, draped in camouflage. Even when it moved, he still tried to explain it. Maybe it was a windmill, without arms, being moved – as they move whole houses in America. Or maybe some film company was making a film, a horror film; it could be, and that would account for the hideous noises too. He simply did not know what to think – so he went on driving towards it.

But when it stepped out on to the road directly in front of him, he jammed on his brakes.

This, he could see, was something new. This had come up all on its own out of the marsh mud. Clumps and tangles of reeds still slithered down its black length, with the slime. As it dawned on him what he was looking at, his head seemed to freeze. That was his hair trying to stand on end. Tears of pure fear began to pour down his cheeks. But he was a photographer – and no true photographer ever misses a chance.

He bundled his camera with him out of the car, snatched off the lens cover, and bowed over the viewfinder.

Blackness filled it. He backed away, swinging the camera from side to side, trying to squeeze the whole huge shape into the frame. But even before he got it full length he saw, in his viewfinder, that it had picked up his car. Aghast, but also overjoyed, he took shot after shot as the great figure slammed his car down on to the road, raised it high and slammed it down again, and again, and again, like somebody trying to beat the dust out of a heavy rug. The birdwatcher remembered, with a fleeting pang, the bittern's eggs. They had been nested in his cap on the passenger seat. But he forgot them as he saw the paint and glass exploding, like steam, each time the car banged down on to the road. Doors flew off, wheels bounded into the reeds, and the mouth in the head opened. As the terrible siren wail came out of that mouth, the birdwatcher turned and ran.

Fast as he ran, he wasn't fast enough. The black, mad giant bounced the twisted, steel-bright tin can of a car into the reeds, then gouged up a handful of marsh mud clotted with weedy roots.

The birdwatcher thought the swamp monster must have caught up with him and kicked him. But it was the flung mass of mud that slammed him from behind, wrapped round him and swept him many yards along the road. He struggled out of it and clutching his greasy camera, spitting out the foul black mire, and sodden, he ran for his life.

When she reached home, Lucy found everything as usual. Her mother had felt no jolts or tremors. She had no idea what her daughter was talking about. Later that evening, when her father came home, he told of the bad smash there had been on the marsh road. A birdwatcher had lost control of his car and gone off the road. He'd gone off his head, too. He had come into the village post office, jabbering all kinds of madness. Police had driven him back into town, where he was staying. Car a total wreck. Funniest thing – every speck of paint was gone off it. And the road was one mess. It looked as if he'd hit the sound barrier. Bit of a mystery.

Listening to this, Lucy wondered what kind of madness the birdwatcher had been jabbering. Maybe those shocks had jounced him off the road and out of his wits at the same moment. She kept remembering that horrible wailing cry. What was going on in the marsh? As she sat there at the table, she watched her arms go goose-pimpled.

Then she began to think about the twisting eel.

2

In Lucy's attic bedroom it was still pitch black. But if she had been awake she would have heard a strange sound – a skylark singing high in the darkness above the house. And if she had been standing in the garden, and looking up into the dark sky through binoculars, she might have seen the glowing, flickering body of the lark, far up there, catching the first rays of the sun, that peered at the bird from behind the world.

The lark's song showered down over the dark, dewy fields, over the house roofs, and over the still, wet gardens. But in Lucy's bedroom it mingled with an even stranger sound, a strange, gasping whimper.

Lucy was having a nightmare. In her nightmare, somebody was climbing the creaky attic stair towards her. Then, a hand tried the latch. It was a stiff latch. To open the door, you had to pull the door towards you before you pressed the latch. If you didn't know the trick, it was almost impossible to open the door. The hand in Lucy's nightmare did not seem to know the trick. The latch clicked and rattled but stayed shut.

Then the latch gave a loud clack, and the door swung wide. On her pillow, Lucy became silent. She seemed to have stopped breathing.

For long seconds the bedroom was very dark, and completely silent, except for the faint singing of the skylark.

Then, in her dream, a hand was laid on Lucy's shoulder. She twisted her head and there, in her dream, saw a dreadful thing bending over her. At first, she thought it was a seal, staring at her with black, shining eyes. But how could it be a seal? It looked like a seal covered with black, shiny oil. A seal that had swum through an oil slick and climbed to

15

her attic bedroom and now held her shoulder with its flipper.

But then she saw, on her shoulder, not a flipper but a human hand. And the hand, too, was slimed with black oil. Then Lucy suddenly knew this was not a seal but a girl, like herself, maybe a little bit younger. And the hand began to shake her, and the girl's face began to cry: 'Wake up! Oh, wake up! Oh, please wake up!'

She cried those words so loud it was almost a scream, and Lucy did wake up.

She sat up in bed, panting. What a horrible, peculiar dream. She pulled the bedclothes around her, and stared into the darkness towards the door. Was it open? She knew the door had been closed, as every night. But if the door was now open . . .

At that moment, wide awake, she heard:

Tap, tap, tap.

On her window.

She listened, not daring to breathe, and it came again:

Tap, tap, tap.

Was it a bird? An early bird? Sometimes little

bluetits came and pecked at the putty around the edge of the window-panes, and peered in. But that was always during the day.

She slid out of her bed and kneeled at the low window, parting the curtains.

At first, she couldn't see a thing. Just blackness. Then, pressing her nose to the glass, she made out the darker roof shapes of the house across the street. And then she noticed something very odd, close to the glass. Something quite small, and dimly white. As she peered, it came closer, till it almost touched the glass.

How could it be what it looked like?

She darted to switch her light on, beside her bed. She paused there, but only a moment, staring at her bedroom door, which was wide open. Then she went back to the window.

Very close to the glass, just outside the window, were three snowdrops. Their stalks were together, their heads hung apart.

How could three snowdrops be flying or floating outside an attic window, so high above the ground?

She tugged the catch down, and opened the window.

The light shining from behind her made the darkness outside seem blacker than ever. But it lit the snowdrops, which were so close. And now she saw they were being held between a gigantic finger and thumb. They came towards her.

She jumped back, and half fell on to her bed. She lay there, staring at the open window. As she stared, the finger and thumb very daintily laid the three flowers on the sill, and withdrew.

Lucy was badly frightened. But, even more, she was curious and excited. Surely this was something wonderful. She must not be afraid. If she let herself be afraid now, what might she miss?

She went forward, and picked up the three flowers. They were real. But where could they be from? Snowdrops in April? Snowdrops were long past.

She peered out into the darkness. And there again, quite close, were the huge finger and thumb – holding a foxglove. A foxglove! In April? Months early?

She reached for it. As she did so, it withdrew. What did that mean? She thought: It wants me to follow.

She remembered her nightmare, and the cry.

And now she could see a gigantic shape towering there in the darkness. It must be standing on their small garden, she thought. Or maybe out on the pavement.

She turned, and began to pull on her clothes.

Lucy eased open the front door and looked out. Her heart was pounding. What was she going to see? A person on top of a vehicle? Or on top of one of those cranes they use for repairing streetlights? Or simply a colossal person with those immense fingers? Whatever it was, the three snowdrops had been real enough. But the street was empty.

Now she was outside, the world seemed not quite so dark. Already, behind the roofs to the east, the inky sky had paled a little. She closed the door behind her and stood a moment, listening. She realized she was hearing a skylark, far up. Somewhere on the other side of the village a thrush sang a first few notes. But the great shape had vanished.

Then something brushed her face lightly and fell to the ground. She picked it up. A foxglove.

19

At the same moment, she smelt a dreadful, half-rotten smell. She knew it straightaway: the smell of the mud of the marsh. She thought it came from the foxglove. But no, it filled the whole air, and she looked upwards.

An immense dark head with two huge eyes was looking down at her, round the end of the house. It must be standing in the driveway, she thought, in front of the garage.

Lucy walked slowly round the end of the house, gazing up. And there it was. Not standing, but sitting – its back to the house wall. And here was the smell all right. This immense creature seemed to be made entirely of black slime, with reeds and tendrils of roots clinging all over. Lucy simply stared up at the face that stared down at her. She felt a wild excitement, as if she were travelling at the most tremendous speed. Had this thing come from the sea, and waded through the marsh? She remembered the face like a seal's in her nightmare, the girl's face with eyes like a seal, and then very sharp and clear that voice crying: 'Clean me.' Had it said: 'Clean me'?

Was this what the snowdrops meant?

Lucy knew exactly what to do. She unrolled her father's hosepipe, which was already fitted to an outside tap, turned the tap full on, and pressed her finger half over the nozzle to make a stiff jet.

It was then she thought she heard another voice, a soft, rumbling voice. Like far-off thunder. She could not be sure where it came from. A strange voice. At least, it had a strange effect on Lucy. It made her feel safe and bold. And she seemed to hear:

'Waste no time.'

The moment the jet hit the nearest leg she saw the bright gloss beneath. It looked like metal – polished black metal. The mud sluiced off easily. But it was a big job. And Lucy was thinking: What are people going to think when it gets light and they see this? She washed the nearest leg, the giant foot, the peculiar toes. She hosed between the toes. This first leg took about as much hosing as an entire car.

The voice came again, so low it seemed to vibrate inside her:

'Hurry!'

21

A faint tinge of pink outlined the chimneys to the east. Already it seemed that every single bird in the village must be singing. A van went past.

Lucy switched the jet to the face. It was an awesome face, like a great, black, wet mudpack. Then the giant hand opened palm upwards, flat on the driveway. Lucy saw what was wanted. She stepped on to the hand, which lifted her close to the face.

The jet sizzled into the deep crevices around the tightly closed eyes and over the strange curves of the cheeks. As she angled the jet to the massively folded shape of the lips, the eyes opened, brilliantly black, and beamed at her. Then Lucy saw that this huge being was a woman. It was exactly as if the rigid jet of water were carving this gleaming, black, giant woman out of a cliff of black clay. Last, she drove the slicing water into the hair – huge coils of wires in a complicated arrangement. And the great face closed its eyes and opened its mouth and laughed softly.

Lucy could see the muddy water splashing on to the white, pebble-dashed wall of the house and realized it was almost daylight. She turned, and saw a red-hot cinder of sun between two houses. A lorry thumped past. She knew then that she wasn't going to get this job finished.

At the same moment, still holding Lucy in her hand, the giant figure heaved upright. Lucy knew that the voice had rumbled, somewhere: 'More water.' She dropped the hose, which writhed itself into a comfortable position and went on squirting over the driveway.

'There's the canal,' she said.

The other great hand pushed her gently, till she lay in the crook of the huge arm, like a very small doll. This was no time to bother about the mud or the smell of it. She saw the light of her own bedroom go past, slightly below her, the window still open, as the giant woman turned up the street.

When they reached the canal, and stood on the bridge looking down, Lucy suddenly felt guilty. For some reason, it was almost empty of water, as she had never seen it before. A long, black, oily puddle lay between slopes of drying grey mud. And embedded in the mud were rusty bicycle wheels, supermarket trolleys, bedsteads, prams, old refrigerators, washing machines, car batteries, even two or three old cars, along with hundreds of rusty, twisted odds and ends, tangles of wire, cans and bottles and plastic bags. They both stared for a while. Lucy felt she was seeing this place for the first time. It looked like a canal only when it was full of water. Now it was nearly empty, it was obviously a rubbish dump.

'The river,' came the low, rumbling voice, vibrating Lucy's whole body where she lay.

The river ran behind a strip of woodland, a mile away across the fields. That was a strange ride for Lucy. The sun had risen and hung clear, a red ball. She could see a light on in a farmhouse. A flock of sheep and lambs poured wildly into a far corner. Any second she expected to hear a shout.

But they reached the strip of trees. And there was the river. It swirled past, cold and unfriendly in the early light. The hand set Lucy down among the weeds of the bank, and she watched amazed as the gigantic figure waded out into midstream, till the water bulged and bubbled past those thighs that

were like the pillars of a bridge. There, in the middle of the river, the giant woman kneeled, bowed, and plunged under the surface. For a moment, a great mound of foaming water heaved up. Then the head and shoulders hoisted clear, glistening black, and plunged under again, like the launching of a ship. Waves slopped over the bank and soaked Lucy to the knees. For a few minutes, it was like a giant sea beast out there, rearing up and plunging back under, in a boiling of muddy water.

Then abruptly the huge woman levered herself upright and came ashore. All the mud had been washed from her body. She shone like black glass. But her great face seemed to writhe. As if in pain. She spat out water and a groan came rumbling from her.

'It's washed you,' cried Lucy. 'You're clean!'

But the face went on trying to spit out water, even though it had no more water to spit.

'It burns!' Lucy heard. 'It burns!' And the enormous jointed fingers, bunched into fists, rubbed and squeezed at her eyes.

Lucy could now see her clearly in full daylight.

She gazed at the giant tubes of the limbs, the millions of rivets, the funny concertinas at the joints. It was hard to believe what she was seeing.

'Are you a robot?' she cried.

Perhaps, she thought, somebody far off is controlling this creature, from a panel of dials. Perhaps she's a sort of human-shaped submarine. Perhaps . . .

But the rumbling voice came up out of the ground, through Lucy's legs:

'I am not a robot,' it said. 'I am the real thing.'

And now the face was looking at her. The huge eyes, huge black pupils, seemed to enclose Lucy – like the gentle grasp of a warm hand. The whole body was like a robot, but the face was somehow different. It was like some colossal metal statue's face, made of parts that slid over each other as they moved. Now the lips opened again, and Lucy almost closed her eyes, she almost shivered, in the peculiar vibration of the voice:

'I am Iron Woman.'

'Iron Woman!' whispered Lucy, staring at her again.

'And you are wondering why I have come,' the voice went on.

Lucy nodded.

'Because of this!' The voice was suddenly louder, and angry. Lucy winced, as the eyes opened even wider, larger, glaring at her.

'What? Because of what?' Lucy had no idea.

'Listen,' rumbled the voice.

Lucy listened. By now, the whole land, inside the circle of the horizon, was simmering and bubbling with birdsong, like a great pan.

'The birds?' she asked. 'I can hear –'

'No!' And the black eyes flashed. A red light pulsed in their depths. Lucy felt suddenly afraid. What did she mean?

'Listen – listen –' The rumbling voice almost cracked into a kind of yell. A great hand had come out now and folded round Lucy's shoulders, just as her father would put his arm around her, while the other hand, with that colossal finger and thumb, just as daintily as it had held the snowdrops, took hold of her hand and gripped it, softly but firmly.

Lucy's fright lasted only for a second. Then she was overwhelmed by what she heard. A weird, horrible sound. A roar of cries. Thousands, millions of cries – wailings, groans, screams. She closed her eyes and put her free hand over her ear. But it made no difference. The dreadful sound seemed to pound her body, as if she were standing under a waterfall of it, as if it might batter her off her feet. Or as if she were standing in a railway tunnel, and the express train was rushing towards her, an express of screaming voices –

Finally, she could stand it no longer and she actually screamed herself. She opened her eyes, trying to drag her hand free and to twist free of the hand enclosing her shoulders. But the thumb and finger held her too tightly, and the enfolding hand gripped her too firmly. And all the time the immense black eyes, so round and so fixed, stared at her. And even though her own eyes were wide open that horrible mass of screams, yells, wails, groans came hurtling closer and closer, louder and louder – till she knew that in the next moment it would hit her like that express train and sweep her away.

But at that moment, the fingers and the hand let her go, and the sound stopped. As if a switch had switched it off.

Lucy stood panting with fear. She almost started to run – anywhere away from where she had been standing. But the great eyes, now half-closed, had become gentle again.

'Oh, what was it?' cried Lucy. 'Oh, it was awful!' She felt herself trembling and knew she might burst into tears. Her ears were still ringing.

'What you heard,' said the voice, 'is what I am hearing all the time.'

'But what is it?' cried Lucy again.

'That,' said the voice, 'is the cry of the marsh. It is the cry of the insects, the leeches, the worms, the shrimps, the water skeeters, the beetles, the bream, the perch, the carp, the pike, the eels.'

'They're crying,' whispered Lucy.

'The cry of the ditches and the ponds,' the voice went on. 'Of the frogs, the toads, the newts. The cry of the rivers and the lakes. Of all the creatures under the water, on top of the water, and all that go between.

The waterbirds, the water voles, the water shrews, the otters. Did you hear what they were crying?'

Lucy was utterly amazed. She saw, in her mind's eye, all those millions of creatures, all the creepy-crawlies, clinging to stones and weeds under the water, with their mouths wide, all screeching. And the fish – she could see the dense processions of shuddering, flashing buckles and brooches, the millions of gold-ringed eyes, with their pouting lips stretched wide – screeching. And the frogs that have no lips – screaming. She suddenly remembered how the giant woman had rubbed her eyes in pain, and she thought of the wet frogs, just as wet and naked as eyeballs, burning – rubbing their eyes with their rubbery almost human fingers. And the eels – that eel. Now she knew. That eel's silent writhings had been a screaming.

'What's happening?' she cried.

The Iron Woman raised her right arm and pointed at the river with her index finger. The ringing in Lucy's ears now seemed to be coming out of the end of that finger. She looked towards where the finger was pointing. The river rolled and swirled, just as before. But now it seemed that a hole had appeared in it, a fiery hole, and she could see something moving far down in the hole.

It was the eel again. Just as she had seen it before, there it was, writhing and knotting and unknotting itself. But it was coming towards her, just as if the fiery hole were a tunnel. It came dancing and contorting itself up the bright, fiery tunnel. Now it was very close to them, in the mouth of the strange hole. She heard a crying, and knew it was the eel. And there were words in the crying. She could almost make them out, but not quite. She strained to hear the words coming from the eel that seemed to be twisting and burning in a kind of fiery furnace. And it did seem to be burning. In front of her eyes it blazed and charred, becoming a smoky, dim shape, a spinning wisp. Then the hole was empty.

But already another form had appeared far down in the fiery hole, coming towards them in a writhing dance.

It was a barbel. It danced as if it walked the water

on its vibrating tail, swaying and twisting to keep its balance. Lucy could see the little tentacles of its beard lashing around its mouth as it jerked and spun in the fiery hole. And the barbel too was crying. It seemed to be shouting, or rather yelling, the same thing over and over. But still Lucy could not make out the words. And again, as she strained to catch the words, the barbel writhed into a twist of smoke and vanished, just as the eel had done. But already, far down inside the hole, she could see the next creature. And this time it was an otter.

Just like the others, the otter came twisting and tumbling towards them, up the fiery tunnel, in a writhing sort of dance, as if it were trying to escape from itself. And as it came it was crying something, just like the eel and the barbel. Again, Lucy could almost hear the words, louder and louder as it danced nearer and nearer, till it spun into a blot of smoke at the hole mouth and vanished.

After that came a kingfisher. This dazzling little bird came whirling and crying till it fluttered itself into a blaze of smoke like a firework spinning on a nail.

After that came a frog. The frog's dance was simply a leaping up and a falling down on its back. Then it scrambled to its feet, leaped up and fell on its back, over and over, as if it were inside some kind of spinning fiery bubble, inside the fiery hole. But its voice came loud and clear, a wailing cry like the same words shouted again and again. But Lucy still could not make out what words those were, till the frog too whirled into smoke.

Then came a squirming thing that Lucy could not make out. Then with a shock she recognized it. It was a human baby. It looked like a fat pink newt, jerking and flailing inside a fiery bubble. But just like those other creatures it came up the fiery tunnel, doing its dance, which was like a fighting to kick and claw its way out of the fiery bubble. This time the crying was not like words. It was simply crying – the wailing, desperate cry of a human baby when it cries as if the world had ended.

Lucy could not bear to see any more. She knew this baby, too, would suddenly burst into flames, blaze into a whirl of smoke and vanish. She dropped her face into her hands. Her shoulders shook as she sobbed.

As she got control of herself, she suddenly thought: This is my nightmare. I'm back in it. If I make a big effort, I'll wake up and everything will be all right. And she looked up.

But if she had hoped to see her attic bedroom with the case of five stuffed owls, it was no good. There in front of her eyes were the black columns of the legs of the Iron Woman. And there was the cold river. And she could feel that strangeness in her ears, that ringing, but fainter now, with the singing of the birds breaking through.

The Iron Woman was gazing out through the trees. 'What's happened?' cried Lucy. 'Oh, what's wrong with everything?'

The rumbling voice shook the air softly all around her. 'Them,' she heard, in a low thunder. 'Them. Them. They have done it. And I have come to destroy them.'

The great black eyes stared at Lucy – black and yet also red, with a dull glow. Then the voice came again, louder, like a distant explosion: 'Destroy them!'

And again, still louder, so the air or her ears or her whole head seemed to split. Her whole body cringed, as if a jet fighter had suddenly roared down out of nowhere ten feet above the tree tops:

'Destroy them!'

Who? Lucy was wondering wildly. Who does she mean? Who are 'them'? And she would have asked, but the Iron Woman had lifted a foot high above the ground and for a frightful moment Lucy thought this huge, terrible being had gone mad, like a mad elephant, and was going to stamp her flat. Then the foot came down hard, and the river bank jumped. The Iron Woman raised her other foot. She raised her arms. Her giant fists clenched and unclenched. Her foot came down and the ground leaped. Her eyes now glared bright red, like traffic lights at danger.

Slowly, the vast shape began to dance, there on the river bank. Lifting one great foot and slamming it down. Lifting the other great foot. She began to circle slowly. Her stamping sounded like deep slow drumbeats, echoing through her iron body. But as she danced, she sang, in that awful voice, as if Lucy were dangling from the tail of a jet fighter just behind the jets:

'DESTROY THE POISONERS.
THE IGNORANT ONES.
DESTROY THE POISONERS.
THE IGNORANT ONES.
THE RUBBISHERS.
DESTROY.
THE RUBBISHERS.
DESTROY.'

She wasn't singing so much as roaring and groaning. She seemed to have forgotten Lucy. It was an incredible sight. The size of several big elephants rolled into one, and now working herself up, every second more and more enraged. And Lucy was thinking: She must mean the Waste Factory. People are always worrying about how the Waste Factory poisons everything. She'll trample the whole thing flat. Nothing can stop her.

Lucy's father worked at the Waste Factory. Everybody worked at the Waste Factory. Only the month before, the Waste Factory had doubled its size. It was importing waste now from all over the world. It was booming. Her father had just had another rise in wages.

At the same time, she thought of the million screams of all the water creatures, and even that human baby, inside the Iron Woman's body. No wonder she was roaring and writhing in that awful dance. All the creatures were screaming inside her, and the sound came out of her mouth as this terrible roar. Everybody within miles must be hearing it. And maybe the Iron Woman truly was going mad in front of her eyes, with the torments of all those burning, twisting, screaming water creatures inside her.

Then Lucy swayed on her feet, the darkness came rushing in from all sides, and she dropped in a faint. And she lay there unconscious, as the earth beneath her jolted and quivered.

3

When Lucy came round, the Iron Woman had vanished. But the deep giant footprints were there. And when she reached home, there was the hosepipe, still squirting over the driveway. As she turned it off, she saw the foxglove. She picked up the foxglove.

Stealthily opening the front door, she could hear her father and mother in the kitchen. She managed to slip up to her attic unseen. Her light was on and her window still open. And there were the snowdrops.

First, she put the snowdrops in a little cup, with water. Next, she put the foxglove in a tall, thin, glass jar, with water. Then she sat on her bed.

What ought she to do? Was this Iron Woman anything like the Iron Man? Lucy had saved a page from a newspaper, with a picture of Hogarth, the boy who was the Iron Man's friend. It told the name of the farm he lived in and the name of the town nearby. She wrote him a letter. In this letter she described everything about the Iron Woman. Three pages. She began it: 'You are the Iron Man expert and I need your help.' And she ended it: 'Please come quickly or the Iron Woman will smash up the factory where my dad works and kill all the people.'

She sellotaped one of the snowdrops to the letter, just beside her signature, and drew a ring round it, with an arrow pointing to the word PROOF. Then she added: 'PS You can camp in our orchard. People do. Say you want to birdwatch in the marsh like lots of people.'

After posting this letter, she started searching for the Iron Woman. Maybe if she knows my father works at the Waste Factory, she thought, she will think again. Or maybe she'll smash it up only after he's come home. After all, I'm her friend. She came to me to be washed. I showed her the river. She showed me the creatures crying. But though Lucy searched for most of that day, she found no trace of the Iron Woman.

She went back again to the river, to look again at those footprints. Their size and depth frightened her more than ever. She thought they might lead somewhere, but they didn't. The Iron Woman must have gone up or down the river, wading in the water, when she left Lucy. Upriver, she would come to the Waste Factory. But she might have gone downriver, back into the marsh or the sea.

That evening, Lucy was relieved when her father got home. Ought she to tell him everything? Then maybe he could warn the factory somehow. By the time she went to bed she had a splitting headache. But still she hadn't mentioned the Iron Woman. She knew she should, but somehow she couldn't. Her mother and father would never believe her. She just knew they wouldn't. They would ask her endless questions. They would think something was wrong with her. They might even want to take her to the doctor.

She hardly slept. She knew she was waiting. She lay there, listening, hearing every slightest sound. She had left her window slightly open, so she would hear better. She kept remembering the creatures and their cry, and that dreadful dance. Gradually, as she thought about it all, she became more and more frightened. Perhaps the Iron Woman really was insane. What did she mean, 'Destroy'? The night hours passed slowly.

The lark began to sing, climbing up through the darkness. As soon as it's light, thought Lucy, I'll start searching again. And with that thought she fell asleep and began to dream.

Just as before, somebody was coming up the attic stair, but this time in a hurry. The door banged open. Once again that strange girl with the oil-slick slime all over her face and hair and arms, was bending over her, with her great black eyes, shaking her shoulder and shouting: 'Quickly. Quickly. Now. Come with me.'

And in her dream, Lucy jumped out of bed.

Immediately the two of them were standing on the marsh road. It was dawn. The red sun hung there, over the marsh, much bigger than the real sun. For some reason, the road was covered with eels, and Lucy thought: Something has frightened them out of the marsh. When she bent to look at one, it stared up at her with human eyes, large, black and shining, like the girl's. She noticed that her own feet were bare, but at that moment the girl grabbed her arm. Lucy looked up. The girl was pointing.

The Iron Woman was rising out of the marsh, beneath the red sun. She reared to her full height, blocking the sun with her black shape. She climbed out on to the road, streaming with slime, and strode away towards the town.

Now Lucy knew what was going to happen. But the Iron Woman was already there and Lucy was too late. She looked around for the girl, but suddenly a mob of screaming women were running past her. The Waste Factory was exploding like a vast bonfire made of firebombs. Huge tangles of pipes soared into the air, roofs rose like wings, buckled and collapsed, in a glare of shooting red flames and blizzards of sparks. The Iron Woman stood in the middle of it, simply tearing the factory buildings out of the ground. She hurled the fragments in all directions, like a madwoman in a strawberry patch ripping up the plants. Lucy stood alone, in her nightdress, her feet bare, knocked and shoved by the stampeding crowd of terrified women.

And now she could see that the Iron Woman herself was on fire. But that didn't stop her one bit. In fact she seemed to enjoy it. She had begun to dance her frightening dance, snatching up girder towers and tossing them aside, kicking gantries into the air, her great black body outlined in her own flames. She was like a giant Guy Fawkes, kicking and trampling and scattering his own bonfire while he blazed.

Now Lucy saw a massive chunk of steel catwalk hurtling towards her through the air. She seemed to have plenty of time to examine it, as it grew larger and larger. Tiny figures of men were clinging to it. She tried to see if one of them was her father. And yes – there he was. She could see him clearly, embracing a girder, his head twisted and staring down at her in amazement as he fell towards her.

She woke with a cry and scrambled out of bed as if that jagged mass of steel rails and girders with its cargo of clinging men might crash on to her pillow. She stood by the window, shaking. She had never had such a nightmare. She hardly dared close her eyes in case the whole thing might still be going on inside there, behind her eyelids.

The morning was perfectly still. She could hear the lark, faint and far up. The window square was dark blue. On the windowsill, just inside the curtain, side by side, the two snowdrops dangled their heads over the edge of the little cup, still fast asleep.

Ever since the Iron Man had made Hogarth so famous, all kinds of people sent him letters. But this was the strangest yet. He sat on his bed re-reading it, and looking at the snowdrop.

He'd often wondered if the Iron Man had any relatives, somewhere. They'd be hidden away, of course. Quite likely in some deep mudhole. Or in the sea. Or inside the earth. After all, the Iron Man had come from somewhere. Why shouldn't there be others?

What puzzled Hogarth was all this about the crying of the creatures, the uproar of screeches coming through the Iron Woman's hand when she touched you. It sounded like electrical voltage. It sounded dangerous. And the Iron Woman herself sounded dangerous. That dance. And that mad song 'Destroy'.

Yes, he had to go. After all, he was the expert Iron Giant handler. Besides, what would the Iron Man make of it? Sometimes, Hogarth thought, the Iron Man seemed a bit lonely. But first, he'd better go and see.

In the holidays it was easy to get away from home for a few days. Those marshes were famous for birds, and Hogarth had been given a pair of binoculars for Christmas. His father wanted some help repairing fences, but then said there wasn't much that needed doing, he could do it himself. His mother drove Hogarth to the station with his packed sandwiches and his tent. By five that afternoon he had pitched the tent in the small orchard behind Lucy's house. Lucy herself showed him just where. Her mother gave him a cup of tea and Lucy offered to show him the ways into the marsh, where the meres of open water were.

Instead, she took him to the river and showed him the footprints. He saw at once they were the real thing. The toes were new. The Iron Man did not have separate toes. Hogarth kept asking: 'How high is she to the knee? How thick is her arm? Compared to your body. How big is her hand?'

It seemed the Iron Woman was just about the same size as the Iron Man. But where was she? The Iron Man liked to stand among trees. Behind the town, where the land rose into rolling low hills, Hogarth could see some woods. Lucy had not yet searched in those woods. They set off.

On the way, they passed the wreckage of the car, in the marsh, and stopped to look at it. Already it was beginning to rust. Hogarth wanted to get out to it, to inspect it. He stepped from clump to clump of reeds.

'Be careful,' cried Lucy. 'It can be deep if you go in.'

'See the holes.' Hogarth pointed from where he was. Lucy saw a row of three jagged holes across the twisted bonnet and wing.

'Her finger holes,' said Hogarth. 'Where she grabbed it.'

Coming back, he made a long stride to a reed clump that collapsed under his foot. With a floundering splash he managed to keep his balance, but he was in over his knees and sinking fast. He lurched another stride or two and was stuck, sinking again. Lucy jumped down the bank and just managed to catch his reaching hand.

But as she began to heave him towards safety they both froze and stared at each other.

'Can you hear it?' she cried. 'That's it.'

Hogarth's mouth opened. He was sinking slowly, but he could not believe his ears. He looked as though he had seen an amazing thing in the sky behind Lucy's head. And she shouted again, above the deafening roar in her own ears:

'That's it. That's their noise. That's the creatures.'

Hogarth made another wild lunge, scrambled up the grassy bank and let go of her. The moment their hands parted the sounds stopped.

Hogarth was panting, as if he'd run across a field.

He looked around wildly, every way.

'Was that it? I heard them all. I could hear them all. I seemed to see things.'

'Isn't it horrible?' cried Lucy. 'Are your ears ringing?'

Hogarth nodded. His eyes were wide open, as if they had no lids. Looking at him, Lucy felt even more frightened. Perhaps it was all far more dreadful than she had thought. Far, far more dreadful.

Suddenly he glared at her fiercely and grabbed her hand. Lucy squeezed her eyes shut as the sound came again – exactly as if it had been switched on like a glaring light full in her eyes. Or like an amplifier full blast into her earphones. It actually seemed to hurt her, like a whacking blow all over her body at the same moment.

He let go of her hand and the sound stopped.

'It's when we touch, don't you see?' he cried. 'It's when we touch.'

Lucy felt bewildered. She was too frightened to think. Hogarth's excitement was frightening. As if the sounds, the screams of all the creatures, weren't bad enough. Hogarth somehow made it worse.

And then again, without warning her, he clasped her wrist again, with his right hand. And again they stared at each other as the shattering din, the howls, the screeches, the wailings, the groans and screams engulfed them. Then they jumped apart, ears ringing.

'Is it in me? Or is it in both of us?' Lucy almost shouted. 'What's happening? We have to find her.'

They set off again. Maybe the Iron Woman could explain what it all meant. Hogarth did not know what to do with his excitement.

'It's contagious!' he cried. 'You've caught it off the Iron Woman. Now I've caught it off you. And if I grab somebody, they'll hear it too. And then if they grab somebody they'll hear it too. And on and on. Just think!'

Lucy didn't dare to think. What was it going to be like when her father touched her, and her mother?

They hurried on towards the woods.

They searched all along the bottom fringe of the woods, but there was no sign of her having gone in, no great footprints.

'Maybe she's just not here any more,' said Lucy.

'Maybe she just came and now she's just gone. Maybe she wasn't real somehow.'

They looked out across the town towards the marsh and the strip of sea, dark in the evening. Hogarth could feel the disappointment creeping up on him.

'No,' he said. 'She was real.'

'But if she's gone,' said Lucy, 'she might just as well not have been.'

Hogarth caught her hand.

Anybody looking at them would have seen nothing but a boy and a girl holding hands under the woodside. But to them it was as if they were trapped in a tunnel flattened against the wall, while an express train went past within inches of their faces.

And now Hogarth saw things quite clearly, as Lucy did. In every cry of the terrific roaring blast it seemed to him that he could see a wild face, a mouth stretched wide, a body hunched up. Even though he was simply gazing at the far edge of the sea, it was as if he were looking through the earth, and seeing it crammed full of every possible kind of creature – all screaming, wailing with all their might, where

51

the tiniest shrimp sounded like a mad elephant and sticklebacks sounded like trapped tigers and slim black leeches like bellowing alligators.

Finally, Lucy snatched her hands away and pressed her palms over her ears.

'Let's see this Waste Factory,' shouted Hogarth. 'Let's have a look at it.'

In the dusk the factory resembled a small, separate city, glowing with a thousand lights. Smoke from thirty chimneys climbed straight up in the still air then flattened out, as if under a ceiling, making a floating carpet over the town beyond. The whole factory throbbed like a vast car engine running under its lifted bonnet. And yet, Lucy knew, inside it was teeming with people.

It had been built outside the town and right beside the river. At first, it had merely crushed old vehicles, for scrap. Then it had begun to recycle waste, of certain kinds. Then it grew bigger, and began to recycle waste of all kinds. Now it collected waste from other countries. It grew bigger, with incinerators burning night and day. It grew bigger, with acres of oildrums, painted all colours and piled in teetering stacks, full of nameless waste from different industries, and different countries. A fleet of articulated trucks came and went constantly, bringing in the waste, or taking waste out to be dumped in other places.

Nearly everybody in the town, and in the villages around, worked there. They called it 'Chicago'.

Lucy and Hogarth stood on the opposite bank. Even in the dimming light they could see the pipes pouring foam out of the factory's side. Lucy counted fifteen pipes. A strange smell came off the river too. Like the bitter taste of a knife blade. But she knew that the smell often changed.

Suddenly, over the drumming of the factory came a new sound. They looked downriver.

What Hogarth thought was a clump of trees seemed to be moving. The sound came again, a roaring wail – like a siren.

'It's her,' hissed Lucy.

They watched as the Iron Woman came wading up the river. Horrified, they saw her reach out and grasp the top of a tall cylinder, which looked like a gasometer enmeshed in pipes and ladders. The screech of tearing metal told them what was happening.

'If she breaks the pipes,' cried Hogarth, 'everything will pour into the river.'

'Iron Woman!' Lucy almost screamed. 'Iron Woman!'

And at once the Iron Woman became still. Then she loomed larger. She stood above them.

'We've been looking for you,' cried Lucy. 'This is Hogarth. He knows the Iron Man.'

The gigantic figure kneeled on the river bank. Her huge face came down, her eyes came close. Hogarth found himself looking into her strange black eyes.

How different! he was thinking. She's really not much like the Iron Man at all. She seems to be differently made.

But what he said aloud was: 'I've come from the Iron Man. He has a plan. He knows what to do.'

Those eyes, it seemed to Hogarth, smiled somehow. And a rumbling became a voice. 'Some plans,' it said, 'are bad.' It sounded just like thunder, coming from everywhere at once and crumbling away into the far distance.

'No, no!' cried Lucy. 'It's a way to stop the rubbishers.'

The great black eyes seemed to grip both of them, and the voice came again. 'They have to be changed,' it said. 'Not just stopped.'

'That's the Iron Man's plan,' cried Hogarth. 'To change them.'

Lucy had no idea what Hogarth was talking about. She only knew she had to stop the Iron Woman ripping down Chicago. And Hogarth had no idea either. He had simply said the first thing that came into his head. But now he'd started he knew he had to go on, even though it was a complete lie.

'The Iron Man is on his way,' he said. 'To help you. He'll be here tomorrow.' He spoke very loud, as if to a deaf person. He was already thinking what he had to do.

The Iron Woman stood erect. Her arm rose and pointed. Her voice rumbled through them: 'Tomorrow I shall be in that wood. If Iron Man does not come, I shall finish what I started. I shall tear this factory out of the ground tomorrow night. Then he can come and eat it.'

The Iron Woman climbed out of the river past them, and disappeared into the dark woods.

'Home,' said Lucy. 'My parents will be worried.'

But as they half walked, half trotted towards Lucy's home, it was Hogarth who was worried. He had to find a telephone.

At last they came to a kiosk. He reversed the charges and gave the number that only he knew. He listened to it ringing. How strange to know that it was ringing actually inside the Iron Man's head.

Then came a click, then silence, then: 'Y-e-e-e-e-e-s.' That funny, familiar voice.

Hogarth told him everything. And he kept repeating: 'You have to come quick – by tomorrow.'

But the Iron Man said nothing more. Hogarth held the receiver, listening into the great silence – the silence inside the Iron Man's head. 'You do hear me, don't you?' he cried.

But suddenly – a click and brrrrr! The Iron Man had switched off.

Hogarth stood for a while. He knew the Iron Man didn't waste words. But would he come or wouldn't he? Had he understood or hadn't he?

Next morning, Hogarth took his binoculars to the marsh. But he waited near Otterfeast Bridge, where Lucy was going to meet him. He sat on the bank, over the drain, spying here and there through his binoculars. After a while, he noticed something floating towards him on the slow current of the drain. It turned out to be a carp – a huge carp as big as a collie dog. He raked it in with a stick and sat looking at it. He had heard that carp were very hard to kill. You could keep them alive for days in a wet sack. But something had killed this. He was counting the big scales when Lucy arrived on the bridge.

'I know what we'll do,' she announced. 'We have to go to the factory and tell them to stop. And if they don't stop pouring out poisons their factory will be pulled down tonight.'

'Nobody will believe that,' said Hogarth. 'They won't take any notice of us.'

'Yes they will,' cried Lucy. 'Because I'll give them the fright.'

'The fright?' asked Hogarth. But then tried to snatch his hand away as Lucy grabbed it. He was too late. Yes, yes, now he realized what she meant. And it was as bad as he remembered. He had to brace himself. It was instantly full blast. It didn't need any warming up. There it was – terrible as ever – as if it had never stopped.

He tore his hand free.

'That will scare them all right,' he gasped, 'if they can hear it.'

'Of course they'll hear it. I'll grab their ears. And you too, you grab them too.'

Hogarth did not say what he was thinking. He was afraid that he might not have the scream power. Maybe only Lucy had it. But then – what if he did have it? He imagined catching hold of some man by both his ears and watching his face as the noise blasted through him, altering his brains.

They set off. Soon they were at the great main gates of Chicago, which stood wide open.

Lucy and Hogarth dodged in past the crush of grinding and banging lorries that seemed to be fighting their way out through the gate and in through the gate at the same time, in clouds of concrete dust.

Lucy was thinking: If I keep telling myself that I know exactly where I'm going and exactly who I want to see – then nobody will stop me.

She pushed in through the plate-glass doors of the main office block directly behind a man in a suit who clutched a briefcase and walked with bounding strides as if he had only seconds to get where he was going. Hogarth followed her just as three men burst out of the lift and came hurtling across the reception hall almost running and out through the glass doors, rearranging their folders and papers in their arms as they went, and talking very loud all three together as if they had planted a bomb on a short fuse somewhere inside the building and were trying to disguise their getaway.

Lucy seemed to know what to do. Hogarth thought:

Well, her dad works here. She knows the ropes. Actually, Lucy had no idea – except to find the Manager's office and go straight there. She looked past the unhappy screen of rubber plants and saw the plan of the office block on the wall. She marched across, past the little fountain and its bowl of plastic lilies, and Hogarth imitated her.

He had enough sense to know that if they glanced towards the receptionist and caught her eye, she would ask them what they wanted – and that would be the end. She would say: 'Please wait over there.' Then she would phone for somebody who would tell them that nobody could speak to them that day. And their attack would have failed. Luckily, she was busy. Hogarth watched her out of his eye-corner, bent over her jumble of computers and fax machines, her hands scrabbling through heaps of papers as if her fingers chased each other. The phone was tucked between her cheek and her shoulder, and the top of her bowed curly head was plainly saying: 'Please don't interrupt me.'

The Manager's office was on the fourth floor.

Hogarth and Lucy went to the open lift. Two men got in beside them. Lucy pressed the button for the fourth, one of the men for the second, the other for the third. Neither spoke to the other. Both stared at Lucy and Hogarth but neither opened his mouth. Both for some reason looked very angry.

Well they might, if they had known what was coming.

A few seconds later Lucy and Hogarth were walking down the blue carpet of the corridor between doors, and there it was, at the end – a brass nameplate:

J. Wells

MANAGER

One knock from Hogarth's knuckle and Lucy walked straight in, Hogarth behind her. He closed the door.

They paused. It was a large, bright room. The whole facing wall was one big window on to the mass of steaming pipes and towers, where half a dozen factories of different kinds seemed to have been jammed into one.

The man sitting behind the desk had his back to them, and was staring out into that jungle of steel while he crowed into a telephone: 'Anything is possible! Absolutely anything is possible. This firm's unspoken motto is "Impossible is not a word." It's as good as done. Right! Right! Yes! Of course! Wonderful! Magnificent! Good!'

Laughing, he turned, put the phone down – and saw Lucy and Hogarth.

He had a large space of face which seemed larger because it went right over to the back of his neck. His eyes, nose and mouth were all pinched together in the middle of it, as if they had been knotted tightly by the little ginger moustache. His ears, Hogarth noticed, were unusually large. Big ears, Hogarth's father would say, mean long life, but Hogarth was also thinking they would be good to grab.

'Who the devil are you?' If the Manager hadn't been so astonished he might have been more polite. Also, he smelt trouble.

But Lucy had already stepped forward. She pointed

her right forefinger straight at the man's moustache, like a pistol.

'Your factory has poisoned the river. It's killed all the fish. It's poisoning all the creatures. It's poisoning the marsh. You have to stop it. Today. Now.'

Her voice really rang out.

The Manager couldn't believe his ears. 'Please get out,' he said quietly, and his hand went to the phone. He was used to this kind of accusation – though not from a wild-faced girl in his own office.

'If you don't stop it, this minute,' Lucy shouted in that strange, solemn voice, 'your factory will be destroyed. I'm telling you, it will be destroyed. Or worse.'

And then she remembered the writhing baby in the tunnel of fire and her voice rose to a yell: 'You're poisoning all the creatures and you're also poisoning me.'

He had picked up the phone. 'John, spot of trouble. Get somebody into my office quick.'

Then he came round the desk. He was a thickset, tough-looking fellow. He had started his career as a scrap-iron dealer, a weightlifter, a lover of hard edges who delighted in pounding big posh saloon cars into small cubes. This is it, thought Hogarth. He's going to throw us out. What do we do now?

But he strode past them and held the door wide.

'Out!' he snapped, without looking at them.

But then something truly amazing happened. Lucy ran at him and grabbed the wrist of the hand that held the door. Hogarth knew what that meant. Even so, he was astounded by the change that came over the Manager's face. It contorted, as if a pan of scalding water had been tipped over his legs.

'Aaaaaaagh!' he screeched. 'Aaaaaaaaaagh!' And he reeled away across the room, with Lucy hanging on to him like a little wolf being dragged by a lumbering moose.

Suddenly another man stood in the doorway shouting: 'What the hell's going on?'

Hogarth saw his chance. I'll give it to him, he thought, right where he can't miss it. And he jumped up to grab the man's ears. The man caught his wrists, but even so Hogarth managed to catch one ear.

And it worked. The man's mouth gaped, as if he had been stabbed in the back. 'O God in heaven!' he bellowed and banged back against the door, trying to get his hands to his quite big ears. But whatever he did, it made no difference, and he began to flail at Hogarth, who closed his eyes and bowed his head, ignoring the blows and simply hanging on. He knew what the man was hearing because he himself could hear it.

It was a very unusual sight there in the Manager's office. The two men writhing and lurching about the room, bouncing off the walls as if they were being electrocuted, like balls in a pin-ball machine, while the girl and the boy clung on and were dragged after.

The shouts brought in others from other offices. All at once Hogarth was struggling and squirming in the hands of two men who lifted him clear of the floor. At the same time a blonde secretary writhed her vivid lips and slapped at his face and head with her bony hands, screaming: 'Little beast! Little beast!'

He got a glimpse of Lucy's legs whirling in the air, and a group of figures wrestling around her.

But whoever touched either Lucy or Hogarth had to deal with the blast of cries – the roar of screams and groans, as if loudspeakers had been clamped over their ears and the tortured cries of the creatures were colliding in the middle of their brains. Even the woman's slaps hit her with bangs of scream.

So it was not just a simple matter of throwing out a girl and a boy who were neither of them very heavy.

In the end, they were thrown out. But not before everybody in the office block had come crowding to see the cause of the uproar, and had tried to get into the action. And whoever touched any of those who had fought with Lucy and Hogarth was hit by the same explosion of screams. It was exactly what Hogarth had called it – instant contagion. Everybody was utterly bewildered. Secretaries who had only been pushed aside staggered away, stunned by what they had heard and glimpsed. And now when they touched each other, there it was again. Nobody knew where the screams were coming from or how they came or why.

The whole shouting mob burst out through the

glass doors at the front of the office block, where Lucy and Hogarth managed to stumble clear. Now Lucy turned, and shouted again:

'Now you know what it's like. That noise is the creatures screaming with your poison. Now you'll never get away from it.'

'Get out of here!' roared the Manager. His collar was burst. His tie was gone. Somehow his jacket sleeve was almost ripped off. All this had happened in his efforts to escape from the screams.

'The police are on their way. They'll settle you people.'

The effect on those office workers was shocking. Secretaries sat sobbing. Men wandered from office to office with staring eyes. Nobody could explain it, and nobody could think of anything else. None of them could escape the fact that when they touched each other both were stunned by the screams. It was as if they had all become high-voltage scream batteries.

And some of them, some more vividly than others, saw things in the screams. As they heard that dreadful

68

outcry, they saw tiny creatures with wide mouths and terrible eyes, clinging to grass or weed or pebbles. They glimpsed the massed faces of fish, as if they were seeing the streaming leaves of a lit-up tree in a big wind at night, with every leaf the face of a fish, trembling as it screamed.

Nothing could explain it. But there it was. They all felt they might be going mad.

In the Manager's office the important people had assembled. The Chief Chemist, the Head of Accounts, the Sales Manager, the Chief Engineer, the Public Relations Officer. They were like people after a mass accident. They simply stared, in a numbed sort of way, or watched the Manager. And he knew he ought to do something. But what could he do?

'Idiots going on about poisons,' he raged. 'What is all this? We follow good industrial practice. We stick to the rules. We spend our lives cleaning up other people's muck and –'

He threw up his hands. But they all knew that this was not just an ordinary protest. What they were all thinking about, and what kept them all so silent, was the thought: If we touch each other again, the screams are there. Those horrible, horrible screams. What are they? And what do they mean?

And two or three were thinking: How long will it last? Will it wear off? What about when I get home and my wife gives me a kiss? What happens when the dog jumps up at me?

They had no idea, of course, that the truly dreadful things had hardly begun.

Lucy and Hogarth walked home in a daze. Her plan had worked too well in a way. But in another way it hadn't worked at all.

'They've all caught it!' cried Hogarth. 'Did you see that man's face? I thought it was going to fly off and out through the window when I grabbed his ears.'

'But will it stop the factory?' Lucy almost frowned.

'It might!' cried Hogarth. 'They've got to think about it. How long do you think it will take before the whole world's plugged into the giant scream? And nobody dare touch anybody else?'

The idea horrified him. At the same time, he

felt like rolling on the ground with laughter. It was horrifying – but also amazing, wonderfully amazing! To think of such a thing!

And Lucy too, she was frightened by everything that was happening. At the same time, she was dazed with excitement. After all, if that was the way things were, that was the way they were.

Her mother and father were less trouble than she had expected. Once she had grabbed their hands and let them hear what everybody was talking about, they sat listening to her. She told them everything. As they listened, they began to feel slightly afraid of their daughter.

'But this business about closing the factory,' her father kept saying.

'Destroying it,' corrected Lucy. 'Not closing it.'

'But people's livelihoods!' he cried. 'Everybody works there. What do you think I'd do?'

'That doesn't bother the Iron Woman,' said Lucy. 'All she thinks about are the screams. Some of those screams are baby screams, you know.'

Her parents stared at her. She reminded them

again of the creatures that had come dancing and writhing up the tunnel of fire. Her mother sighed and rested her forehead on her hands. She stared down at the table.

'How do you come to be mixed up in all this?' shouted her father. 'Why you?' The wrinkles on his brow were a new, unfamiliar shape. His hair was tousled, as if he had just got out of bed in the middle of the night.

'The Iron Man will know what to do,' said Hogarth. He wanted to make Lucy's parents feel better. But now they turned their stare on him, with the same dreadful, anxious look. Blackish rings had appeared under their eyes. And Hogarth was thinking: Is this how people look during a war? – when there came a knock on the door.

'The police!' gasped Lucy's mother, looking more haggard than ever.

'Why should it be the police?' cried Lucy. 'I'm not going tearing up any factory. I'm not the Iron Woman.'

Her mother opened the door. Three journalists

stood there from the local newspapers. And as they introduced themselves, others, behind them, were getting out of cars.

The family managed to get to bed finally, but none of them could sleep. Their brains were spinning. They would be headlines in the morning. And before noon the television people were coming.

Lucy had put the cup with the snowdrops and the vase with the foxglove beside her bed. She fancied she could see the snowdrops glowing slightly in the dark. Though the journalists had asked a thousand questions, she had never mentioned the Iron Woman. They had gone off thinking it had all begun with her – Lucy. All they could think was: This girl has abnormal powers. And they argued with each other about different explanations.

Hogarth lay in his tent, listening to the orchard and the darkness. Everything was so silent now, he thought he could hear the stars rustling. How could the whole globe seem so silent with that terrible scream, somehow, still going on. He took hold of his

left wrist with his right hand. Silence. It needed two people to plug into the scream. Then a tawny owl hooted, just above his tent, and his hair went icy. He curled up and pulled his sleeping bag over his head. And suddenly he was thinking of the Iron Man. He imagined him coming across the country in a straight line. So he fell asleep dreaming about the Iron Man, who seemed to grow, till he was far bigger than the Iron Woman, as he strode through the night, over trees and houses, with the moon glistening on his metal.

4

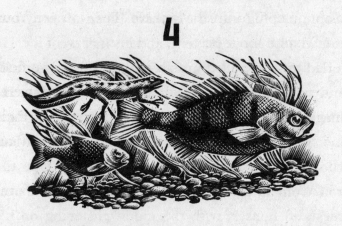

Next morning Hogarth and Lucy were up early. They planned what they were going to do. Lucy left a note for her parents:

> When the TV people come to interview
> me, tell them I'll be at the factory gate
> at 12 o'clock sharp.

Soon they were climbing up towards the woods behind the town. They scrambled over a brambly bank and were among the trees.

'Look!' hissed Hogarth. He was pointing at the

ground. Lucy gazed at the deep, huge prints in the soft mould. 'The Iron Man. No toes, you see. Your Iron Woman has toes.'

The track led up through the woods to the field above, that climbed to a hilltop. And there they were, sitting facing each other, two colossal figures, their backs to the boles of great cedars that grew among the ancient stones on the hill's very crown.

'We're here,' yelled Lucy, and ran towards them. 'It's us.'

The immense heads turned.

'Iron Man!' shouted Hogarth. 'I knew you'd make it.'

Lucy told them everything that had happened: the fight in the offices, the journalists, the television crew coming today. The enormous eyes glowed. The Iron Man's glowed amber. The Iron Woman's glowed black. But not a sound came out of either of them.

'Why don't you come and let the TV people see you?' cried Hogarth. 'You could give them the screams, on television. Then they'd have to believe. Everything would have to change.'

'Oh yes, you must come,' cried Lucy. 'Just the sight of you –'

A humming started up within the Iron Woman. 'Nothing would change,' came the deep, rumbling, gentle voice.

Lucy and Hogarth stared at her. What did that mean? Weren't the screams going to change everybody? And the sight of the Iron Woman, as a giant scream transmitter – wouldn't that change everything?

'It needs something more,' said the great voice, up through their shoe-soles.

Hogarth and Lucy were baffled. How could there be anything more?

'So what do we do?' asked Hogarth.

The rumbling started again. And the voice came again: 'Do?' Then again, louder: '*Do?*' Then, with a roar: 'DO?'

And Lucy and Hogarth almost fell over backwards as the Iron Woman, in one terrific heave, got to her feet. Branches were torn off as she rose erect among the cedars. And her arms rose slowly above her head. Her fists clenched and unclenched, shooting her

fingers out straight. Then clenched again. She lifted one foot, her knee came up, then:

BOOM!

Her foot crashed down. The whole hilltop shook and the sound echoed through her great iron body as if it were a drum. Again, her other foot came up – and down:

BOOM!

Ripping the boughs aside, her fists clenching and unclenching, her feet rising and falling, Iron Woman had begun to dance. There in the copse, in a shower of twigs, pine cones, pine needles and small branches, she revolved in her huge stamping dance, in front of the Iron Man whose eyes glowed bright gold. And she sang, in that deep, groaning, thundering voice of hers: 'Destroy the ignorant ones. Nothing can change them. Destroy them.'

She went on repeating that over and over, in time to her pounding footfalls, as she turned round and round. Lucy hid her mouth behind her clenched fists. The Iron Woman was terrifying. She was overwhelming. She was tremendous.

'Give them a chance,' Lucy screamed. 'Let's see what they say today. They might have changed already.'

She just yelled it out at the top of her voice. Her father was one of the ignorant ones, according to the Iron Woman. But it was no good. The giant dancer's eyes were glowing a dark red. She stamped each foot down as if she wanted to shatter the whole leg.

'Nothing will change. Only their words change. They will never change. Only their words change. Only their words only their words only their words . . .'

Then her voice became simply a roar. And now it seemed to Hogarth that inside her roar he could hear the scream, the wailing and the crying of all the creatures, roaring out over the woods. And again he began to see the faces, large, small, tiny – the wide mouths and the terrible eyes of the SCREAM.

But now the Iron Man was getting up. And he suddenly spoke. His voice was not so loud as the Iron Woman's, but it was harsher, more piercing.

'I have an idea.' And he held up his arm.

The Iron Woman had stopped. Slowly, she lowered her arms, but her eyes, fixed on the Iron Man, glowed red as ever.

'Destroying them is no good,' he said, in his dry, grating voice. Lucy heard all the cogs in it. They were stiff, because he spoke so rarely. 'You could not destroy them all,' he went on. 'And everything would be rebuilt as before. New factories, the old poisons. New people, the old stupidity. Nothing would be changed.'

The Iron Woman's eyes darkened. And down below, close to the ground, the two pairs of human eyes stared up, round as the eyes of two rabbits.

'Listen to me now,' said the Iron Man.

But instead of speaking, he took the Iron Woman's hand, and seemed to listen.

'Just as I thought,' he said. 'The scream is terrible. And yet it needs something extra.'

Then he took the Iron Woman's other hand with his other hand, so he was holding both her hands in his. All this time he must have been hearing the cry of the creatures through her hands. Now he craned his head backwards and looked up into the sky. Lucy could see that his eyes, too, had become red, and so fierce that a red beam went up from them – quite clear and strong even in the bright morning light.

For two or three minutes nothing happened.

'What's he doing now?' whispered Hogarth.

But Lucy was looking up at the sky. Only a little patch of blue showed, away to the south. The rest was cloud, but quite bright. An even, crumpled layer. And yet something funny was going on, directly above. It looked like a darker dot, spinning.

'Is that a bird?' whispered Lucy, pointing up.

No, it was a small, dark cloud. Already it seemed to have an odd shape. It seemed to be lowering a strange, spinning wisp of itself. A spinning tail of cloud. And the whole cloud seemed to be growing, as it came lower, and lower. It looked like the pictures of a waterspout at sea. But it wasn't whirling upwards, it was spiralling downwards, worming its way towards them.

As it came, they heard a faint roar, like the far-off sound of a big aircraft behind the clouds. That is what Hogarth thought it was. But then he realized the sound was coming from that whirling corkscrew of gloom as it descended, louder and louder.

And now the tip of it was only just above the Iron Woman's head. There it stayed for a while, like a long spinning top, writhing and roaring. Or like a machine drill about to be lowered. The roar was now stupefying, like the roar of a jet plane as it swings towards the runway for takeoff. Lucy and Hogarth covered their ears. The din was painful.

And now it seemed they could see something strange in the spinning cone. As if it kept stopping – just for a moment, like a skater spinning on the toe of one skate who stops just for the fraction of a second at each revolution. And just as you get a fleeting but quite clear glimpse of the whirling dancer's face, in that momentary stop, so now Lucy and Hogarth saw, in the towering tornado cloud, scales.

Scales!

Yes, there it was, just a glimpse – then another, and another. Scales!

But now the most astonishing thing of all happened.

That spinning dark column of scales touched the Iron Woman with its drill point. It touched the top of her head.

Immediately her body seemed to begin to disappear. Actually it began to vibrate. Her body became a blur of vibration. The Iron Man's hands, which still gripped hers, also disappeared in a blur.

As she vibrated, that whirling tower of darkness and scales was pouring into the Iron Woman. And as it poured into her, she seemed to grow.

For minute after minute it went on. More and more darkness came down the spinning cone. The blurred mass of the Iron Woman grew bigger and began to glow blue. And still it went on. Till they saw the upper end of whatever it was lashing about in the sky like a great tail. Still pouring down into the Iron Woman, it was coming to an end.

The roar grew screechier. Suddenly, with a thin, ripping scream like an express train piling into a tunnel too small for it, that lashing tail dived into the Iron Woman and vanished. The instant silence was shocking.

Her shape had reappeared, but now twice as big as it had been, and glowing blue, like the glass of a blue lamp. The Iron Man, his arms reaching up, still held her hands. As they watched, she darkened, and as she darkened, she shrank. At last, she was her normal size again and the Iron Man released her.

'Now,' he said, grinding his voice box, 'now you have all the power of the Space-Bat-Angel-Dragon, my mighty slave from the depths of the universe. It has packed itself inside you. It has become your power.'

The Iron Woman did not move. She seemed stunned by what had happened to her. Her eyes were half closed, gazing at the Iron Man who now spoke again:

'Whatever you want to do, you can now probably do it. The power of the Space-Bat-Angel-Dragon is almost infinite. Be careful what you wish for – because now it will come true. Its power,' said the Iron Man, 'is unearthly.'

The Iron Woman laughed softly. She laughed again, more strongly, a rumbling low laugh. She laughed again, louder. Then she turned, abruptly, and gazed out over the woods, towards the town. Lucy could see she had obviously made up her mind about something.

'What will you do?' she cried. Lucy was thinking of her father, she was suddenly afraid of what the Iron Woman might do to him, along with his workmates.

The Iron Woman looked down at her. Instead of black, or red, her eyes were now deep, dark, fiery blue. And all her body, it seemed to Lucy, was blacker – so black it seemed almost blue. But the Iron Woman only said: 'It is almost midday. Go and give your interview. To the television crew. At the gate of the factory.'

And again she laughed her rumbling, strange laugh that seemed to sink away into the earth.

Lucy and Hogarth set off down the hill.

Minutes later, they saw the TV vans, the cameras, and the small crowd waiting for them at the factory gate, and their hearts sank. This was going to be difficult.

'Remember the scream,' said Lucy.

5

The interviewer was a beautiful young lady famously known as Primula. Her hair swung about, long, blonde, shining, thick. Her made-up face dazzled like a tropical fish. She was known to be fearless. Politicians and celebrities were afraid of her questions. The crowd stared, seeing her so close and alive. Every second, more people collected.

She had listened while three men from the factory had given their descriptions of what was happening. And the Manager, Mr Wells, had promised to speak to her later. She felt more and more excited but also more and more uneasy. What exactly was this terrible scream they were all talking about? So far she had managed to avoid being touched by anybody who carried it. But the more she heard about it the less she liked it.

'Here they are now,' cried the Accounts Clerk, who had been describing to her how, the night before, when he got home, his wife had met him with a kiss – and fainted. And how his little two-year-old son had grabbed at his legs, then fallen screaming to the floor, and then had gone on screaming, because every time his father touched him to comfort him the roar of creatures' screeches and wails had blasted the child again. And how it had got worse when his wife recovered. The first thing she did was to pick up the screaming child, to comfort it, and then, of course, they both got it again – he from her and she from him. They had all become scream batteries. It was absolutely horrible. And other people were the same.

Something had to be done about it.

Listening to this, all Primula could think about was – what was going to happen to her if she too became a scream battery. Her famous baby was only two months old. And her husband was a doctor, touching people all day long. It did not bear thinking about. Television had never shown anything like this, but she wished she'd never come near the place. How was she going to get out of it?

And now here were the two who began it all. Just a pale little girl and a funny gawky boy. Nevertheless, probably the scream-power in them was terrific. Primula watched them warily as they came nearer. But Lucy and Hogarth were just as wary of Primula. Her red lips stretched like sponge rubber when she smiled. They felt like woodland wild animals when her fine, rich perfume reached them.

They had made up their minds what to say. No matter what questions they were asked, they were going to tell the TV cameras just what the factory was doing – dumping poisons not only into this river but all over the land, and importing poisonous wastes from other countries to dump somewhere, all ending up in the living creatures of the rivers, the land and the sea. No matter what this tall, glittering insect of a lady was going to ask them, that's what they were going to tell her camera.

And those people with their tape recorders from radio, and those journalists from newspapers, all crowding to listen – that's what they were going to get. And, Lucy had decided, at some point she was going to grab Primula's arm and give her the full scream.

Primula was already introducing them to the camera. 'What are your names?' she asked, in her famous voice, and her sound recorder held his furry microphone near their faces.

Lucy began to speak. She didn't give her name. She knew she had to say everything the Iron Woman wanted her to say. She kept thinking of all those creatures – all those wide-stretched mouths and dreadful eyes. And those creatures in the fiery tunnel of light. Hogarth stood amazed at the stream of words that poured so fiercely from his new friend.

Primula tried to get in a question. 'But tell us about those strange screams.'

Lucy simply ignored her, and at last Primula let her go on. After all, it was quite a sight, watching this little girl in such a fury. And it would all make sense in a minute, when they got to the scream.

But as she spoke, Lucy had the strangest feeling. She felt as if nobody believed her. It needed something more. Primula was listening, but with a smile on her face. She frowned a little, but mainly she was smiling. Lucy fixed her eyes on that blue sleeve, just above the elbow, and edged a little closer. At that moment a man came pushing through the crowd.

It was the Company Secretary, the man who had helped the Manager and who had grabbed Hogarth. He looked extremely angry and he was shouting.

'Excuse me, I think you may be talking to the wrong people –'

Lucy stopped, and Primula turned towards the new voice. As she did so, her eyes widened. The man's eyes had widened too. In fact, they had become perfectly round. As they watched, his face went dark and his mouth, opening and closing, became enormous. Then he fell to the ground at Primula's feet. Everybody stepped back as he writhed there, on the concrete, like a gigantic eel. At the same time, everybody saw him slither out through his collar. He actually had become a giant eel! His trousers and jacket lay flat and crumpled. A six-foot-long eel, as thick as a man's neck, lay squirming, knotting and unknotting, flailing its head this way and that, snapping its jaws which were the size of an Alsatian dog's – and truly were very like an Alsatian dog's.

Right there, in front of their eyes, the Company Secretary had become a giant eel.

Primula let out a tiny choking cry and collapsed. Her cameraman could not believe his luck. His camera zoomed in on her carefully painted face, with its bluish eyelids closed as if asleep, her hair spread out on the rough old concrete. From there it panned to the gnashing, glaring face of the great eel, only a yard from her. The newsmen's cameras blazed. One of the journalists held a microphone close to the pointed snout.

'Can you tell us what it feels like –' he began, in that half-shouting, jerky voice used by interviewers, '– aaaaaaaaagh!' The eel had clamped its jaws over both the microphone and his hand. He tore his bleeding hand free and staggered backwards. Others pulled Primula to her feet and she began to stare around woozily.

Now the eel, as if it knew exactly what it was doing, writhed on to the grass and away like a snake towards the river. Its tail flipped in the air as it went in.

The whole thing had taken barely a minute. All the journalists began to jabber at each other. Primula had suddenly recovered and was yelling at her cameraman: 'Did you get any footage?'

The cameraman was busy filming the flat, forlorn-looking suit of clothes lying there. He held a long close-up on the empty shoes, one with a fancy red and yellow patterned sock still draped emptily over its side.

'Incredible!' came the shouts. 'Unbelievable! What's going on in this town?'

Lucy and Hogarth watched it all without a word. They were as astounded as everybody else. But now Lucy suddenly shouted:

'Look what's coming!'

While all this had been going on, the Manager,

Mr Wells, had been holding a meeting with the owners and manager of an international firm called Global Cleanup. This firm did nothing but transport poisonous wastes from one country to another. Whoever had a problem getting rid of their wastes, Global Cleanup stepped in and did the job. They found all kinds of ways of making the stuff disappear. Some they dumped in far-off countries, where nobody protested. Some they dumped in the sea. Some they dumped in rubbish dumps. Some down old mine shafts. Some in large holes under fields which they simply dug wherever they could persuade a farmer to let them. And some they burned.

Now they were signing an agreement with Mr Wells. They would pay him £1 per tonne if he would get rid of one million tonnes of special chemical poisonous waste. A million tonnes!

They were sitting round his desk. He had just signed the agreement and was now staring at the cheque. It was the first time he had ever seen £1,000,000 written on a cheque. A waitress was pouring drinks. After that, it would be lunch in the boardroom.

Mr Wells raised his glass of malt whisky.

'Here's to Global Cleanup,' he cried.

'To Global Cleanup!' they chanted in chorus, and with big smiles raised their glasses towards Mr Wells. Then they all put back their heads and drank.

But as they lowered their glasses and squashed the fiery drink over the back of their tongues, the four men from Global Cleanup saw an impossible thing. They saw Mr Wells's face go purplish, like a ripe fig. His glass tumbled and rolled over the table, and at the same time he too flopped forward, chest down over the cheque he had been admiring. Four chairs fell over backwards as the men scrambled to their feet. Was Mr Wells having a heart attack? Or a fit? No, this was no longer Mr Wells.

'My God!' cried the Global Cleanup Sales Chief. 'It's a catfish! And what a catfish!'

All four stared at the broad, blunt, purplish, glistening head sticking out of Mr Wells's burst white collar. They saw the tiny eyes, which looked like buttons of the same stuff as the skin. And they saw the tentacles writhing round its lips.

Then it lurched, with a ponderous, coiling fling, and there was the whole fish, still inside Mr Wells's shirt and jacket, lying across the table. His trousers had fallen off, with his shoes and socks. It slammed its tail down hard and gaped two or three times.

One of the four panicked and ran straight at the wall which stopped him with a bang. Then he tried to climb the wall, bringing down a long picture of the factory on top of himself.

At the same time, the other three became aware of screams, shouts, wild commotion in the offices along the corridor. The door clashed open and Mr Wells's secretary ran in. She was escaping from something. She did not try to explain, she simply screamed. Beyond her, two big sea lions wrestled to get past each other, away down the corridor, bellowing: 'Woink! Woink!'

Then the secretary saw the catfish and with a wail collapsed on the floor, where she huddled sobbing.

The four men dashed out but then halted at the door. Screaming and sobbing secretaries ran in all directions. Junior executives with staring eyes and strange, wild spiky hair shouted at each other. One embraced a writhing sturgeon the size of himself. He was a man with a cool head:

'This is Mr Plotetzky!' he cried. 'We have to get him to water. Help me get him to the river.'

A first-class idea! The four men from Global Cleanup grasped what was happening. 'Explanations later!' cried one. 'Get Mr Wells to the river.' They crushed back through the office doorway as a knot of enormous eels burst out from one office and rolled down the corridor, lashing tails.

All over the building, staff were collapsing on to flippers and thrashing about, knocking over waste-paper baskets and filing cabinets.

'To the river!' was the cry. 'Janice! Daphne! Grab a tail will you!' 'Jane, can you manage?' 'Help, Joanna, help!'

Pandemonium is a poor word for that uproar and confusion. Glass shattered from doors, office furniture staggered and toppled, as slim secretaries struggled with man-sized barbels, carp, salmon and pike, tripping over the litter of empty shoes and tangling,

empty trousers. The seals, giant frogs, colossal water beetles helped themselves, and so did the big eels.

The factory's entire office personnel lurched, flopped, thumped and slithered towards the exit. 'To the river! To the river!'

Like a mob bursting on to the pitch at the end of a football game, they burst out through the front of the office block.

This was what Lucy had seen when she pointed.

'I can't believe it!' screeched Primula. 'Camera! Camera!' And she began to yell and pant into her microphone as the mixed and struggling mass of giant fish and people and humping water beasts surged towards them.

That was only the first wave. The second wave was much bigger – the factory workers. Here they came, the same mixture – men reeling under the weight of huge fish that had been their workmates.

The river boiled as the heavy bodies flung themselves in, or slithered in, churning and swirling. The men who carried their friends did not escape. As soon as they had dumped their fishy fellow workers into the river, they simply fell in after them, changing in mid-air. The river was a heaving mass of clothes and great dorsal fins as the fish squirmed free.

'Oh, get them as they change! Oh, get them half-man half-fish,' screamed Primula to her cameraman. 'Get their faces at the actual moment of change – what a stupendous sight! Never before! It's a first! Look at that! Get that horror – oh, gorgeous! Get that terror in their eyes! Wonderful!'

But now it was beginning to dawn on those who watched all this that only the men had changed. Not a single woman had changed. The film crew, too, and the journalists, were all still as they had been, staring down at the dark, beaky faces, the great hard mouths opening and closing, the round astonished eyes. The giant water creatures could not come out. Nor did they want to go away. They bobbed at the river's edge, along the concrete of the riverside walkway, lifting their heads out and even resting their chins on the concrete, gaping silently, sometimes gasping a dry croak, then rolling under to breathe, while the secretaries and canteen women and aroma chemists gazed down, and the scaly long bodies swirled and heaped in the foamy suds of the river.

'If that water hurt the Iron Woman's eyes,' said Lucy, 'think what it's doing to theirs, and to their gills.'

Even as she said that, a great catfish hurled itself into the air, shaking its head. Then a giant barbel. Then a sturgeon. Soon there were three or four fish in the air at any moment, shaking their gills and contorting their bodies, while eels rocketed out of the water and speared under again.

'They're trying to get away from the water,' said Hogarth. 'But they can't.'

'The river water's poisoning them,' cried Lucy to Primula. 'You know what I told you. Look at them. It's poisoning them.'

'She's right,' cried Primula, 'it's a river of tortures! Just look at them. Get that!'

Her cameraman needed no telling. The news cameras too were flashing non-stop. And the great bewildered fish reared up and plunged under, or lolled their heads along the concrete edge for as long as they could manage before they had to duck back under to breathe the poisonous water, unable to close their lidless eyes in the stinging chemicals.

If Primula had seen more than she ever thought possible, she was now in for the biggest shock of all.

'Look, oh, look!' she heard. Some woman cried the words. And Primula could tell, by the dreadful sound of disbelief in the voice, that something truly unthinkable was now coming. She twisted her head round. An arm was pointing. And then she saw up there, right above her – the Iron Woman.

For a moment, all the women, the cameraman, the journalists stared. Then a strange sighing gasp went up.

The Iron Woman looked awesome, so close, towering above them. And behind her, the Iron Man. Then everybody heard the thunderous words:

'Stop the factory. Let the river run clean. Or all these creatures will die.'

The booming and rumbling voice seemed to go right through their bodies.

'She's right,' came a voice. 'Stop the factory.'

All these women suddenly realized there was something they could do. 'Stop it now. Stop all that stuff going into the river. That's a start!'

But then came another shout, a man's voice:

'It can't be done. I cannot allow that.' Of all the men who had worked at the factory, one was still there in his human form. The Chief Engineer.

'You're the very one we want,' a woman shouted. 'You can show us how to stop it.'

'I cannot allow it,' he told them. He sounded very stern. 'We simply cannot afford –'

Women's hands grabbed him by the throat, by the hair, by the arms. He was half carried and half dragged back into the factory. And those women didn't waste any time. If he hadn't told them exactly what to do, they would have torn him into ragged fragments, like a great doll.

And so, within the hour, the whole factory came to a stop. All power was turned off. Everything closed down.

'This will cost a fortune,' wailed the Chief Engineer.

'Half the plant will be ruined. You can't just switch everything off, you know, and hope for the best.'

'Oh yes we can,' cried those women. 'We've done it.'

'I shall have to make a detailed report –' he began.

But before he got any further he flopped to the ground, with a huge pike's head sticking out of his collar and his clothes wrapping around him like a baggy sack. His bright flat eyes jerked this way and that.

'Into the river with him,' came a cry. 'Let him drink his poisons.'

And so the women carried him to the river, and slid him out of his clothes into the weltering mass of streaming bodies, where he vanished with a loud whack of his broad tail.

Was that the end of it? It was not. Not by a long way.

Not just all over the town, but all over the country men had turned into giant fish, giant newts, giant insect larvae, giant water creatures of some kind. Every man over eighteen years old was in water. And if their eighteenth birthday came on that day, down they flopped with the cake in their mouths.

Wherever the women could not get their husbands into the rivers or reservoirs or ponds, they got them into baths and swimming pools. Nearly every bath in the land had a record-sized barbel, or pike, or some other man-sized fish in it. Or a huge water flea. Here and there it was a monster leech. Mr Wells the giant catfish was now in the swimming pool at his large new home. His two little sons spent their time digging worms and dropping them in, to see him sucking them up off the blue tiles with his great blunt mouth.

The Prime Minister himself was a six-foot-long dragonfly larva, in the bath at Number Ten. His secretary came in every hour to tell him about the latest phone calls, but all he did was wave his feelers at her and push his strange mechanical jaws in and out. Lucy's father was a giant newt. Her mother had collected him from the river in the car, and now he was in the bath. He had to curve his jagged, high-crested tail slightly, to fit in. She was feeding him with cat food. That was a big problem, feeding these creatures, especially those still in the rivers.

Hogarth phoned home. His father was a shiny green frog, with a pulsing throat. He was down in the boggy rushes by the duckpond.

It was a national disaster, of course. The rest of the world was dumbfounded. The sights on their televisions were very hard to believe. At first, experts flew in from other countries to help keep things going. But the moment they stepped off their plane at the airport – down they flopped. The frogs could get back, and the seals, and even the carp if their clothes were well soaked and the flight was not too long. But the other fish had to stay in the nearest water. So that was the end of that. The women had to manage on their own.

Very quickly, everything came to a stop. Electricity failed. So all computers went dead. All TVs went blank. Petrol ran out, the pumps at service stations no longer worked. Telephones went dead. There was no longer any question of Hogarth going home, unless he walked. All food in the shops was soon bought up, and all the candles.

Lucy's mother was distraught. 'What's going to

happen?' she cried. 'We can't live on worms and rainwater. And what will happen to your poor father?' Lucy and Hogarth felt desperate too. The whole thing had got out of hand. Soon it would be famine. Even if other countries dropped food by parachute. The Iron Woman surely didn't want that.

They climbed the hill, up through the wood. The Iron Woman had to help. She'd done it. Now she would have to undo it.

'Maybe people have been taught a lesson,' said Hogarth. 'Maybe she's done enough. Maybe she'll change everybody back, now.'

But the strangest things of all were still to come.

6

There they were, the two familiar figures, sitting facing each other among the stones and the great cedars on the hilltop. Lucy and Hogarth told them how things were. And how everything was getting worse by the minute. How people would soon be starving to death. But the great eyes in the great faces stared down at them without moving. Then the Iron Woman's voice rumbled through them.

'They still haven't learned,' it said. 'The people will have to learn. And change.'

'Oh, they have, they really have,' cried Lucy. 'People are in a terrible state.'

'I shall know when they've changed,' said the Iron Woman. 'Something will happen. A certain thing will happen.'

'What?' asked Hogarth. 'How shall we know what it is?'

'You'll see,' said the Iron Woman. 'Or maybe I should say, you will hear.'

What did she mean?

And at that very moment the Iron Man raised his huge finger.

'There it is now.'

Lucy and Hogarth listened. At first they could hear nothing. Then, without hearing anything in particular, they were hearing something. Like a shuddering in the air.

The Iron Woman got to her feet. The Iron Man stood up beside her. The two of them stood very still, gazing out over the landscape, listening.

'Isn't it the sea?'

Hogarth could hear it now, like a sighing groan. A groan, followed by a groan, followed by a groan. Each time louder. It was as if something were coming

towards them across the country, groaning as it came. Whatever it is, thought Hogarth, it must be vast, almost like the sea.

The Iron Woman raised her right arm and pointed.

A low, webby cloud, almost like a dark mist, had spread over the land. Were the groans coming out of that cloudy mist? As they watched, the cloud seemed to be growing, thickening, bulging into lumps, like a sea of porridge. At the same time it was like nets tangling and untangling. It covered the town and the marsh. It heaped nearer. All the time the groans, like some weary creature groaning with every breath, grew louder, and nearer.

They did not see, they could not see, what was happening beneath the cloud.

Lucy's mother had just had a new shock. Every two hours or so she would go into the bathroom to have a few words with her husband. Not that he ever answered. There he lay, very black, along the bottom of the bath, perfectly still, until she tapped the bath's edge. Then he seemed to wake up. With a slow half-wriggle he would lift himself off the bottom, and his bulging eyes would break the surface. Then he would lie, half-floating, his orange chin on the bath's edge, gazing at her while she tried to cheer him up.

It was hard for her, looking at those cold, round, gold-ringed eyes, to think that this was Charles, her husband.

But this time, when she opened the door a gloomy fog billowed out in her face. It wasn't smoke. Or at least it had no smell. It was a strangely clinging fog, like drifting webs. She brushed it from her face and her hand seemed to be draped with it for a moment. A peculiar clinging gloom, as dark as the smoke of burning tyres, so she could not see the opposite wall of the bathroom. It flowed out around her, past her into the house.

Then she saw that it was rising in puffs from the bath, like a smoke signal. And now she saw the bubbles wobbling up from the mouth of the giant newt – or from her husband's mouth, rather – where he lay, a jagged black shape against the white porcelain, resting lightly on his spread, rubbery fingers.

She tapped the bath, but he ignored her. About every three seconds another fat bubble wobbled up and burst in a dark puff. Like a soft, silent shellburst of those weird, untangling fibres of gloom. She rolled back her sleeve, plunged her hand into the water, and rocked him gently. He still ignored her, only letting out three big bubbles together.

Was he ill? Were these bubbles the beginning of the end? 'Charles!' she called. 'Charles!'

Then she almost screamed it: 'Charles!'

She lifted him up to the surface. It wasn't difficult in the water. Before this, she had always been afraid to touch his bright orange, black-speckled underside, as if it might be poisonous. But she gave no thought to that now. She drew his chin over the bath's edge. He rested there, his eyes fixed and glassy. Another bubble swelled slowly from his lips, till it popped with a tangling puff of gloom. Then, with a wriggle, he backed off and sank to the bottom. Another bubble came up.

Whatever was going on, he seemed to be concentrating on his bubbles.

114

She ran through the bedrooms, which were now dense with the strange gloom, and opened all the windows. She saw Mrs Wild, her neighbour across the street, doing the same thing, with the gloom billowing out around her from the opened windows. Mr Wild was an enormous freshwater shrimp, and he was in the bath too.

'Is he bubbling?' she called. 'Charles is bubbling these funny dark bubbles.'

'What next?' cried Mrs Wild. 'I think I'm going mad.'

In every home it was the same. And in the swimming pools, the water tanks, the ponds, wherever the changed men lay they were burping those bubbles. And all over the land, that dark, ropy, webby fog was rising from the mouths of these dumb creatures – like tangling smokes from countless little campfires.

It rose, forming that dark cloud, that eerie, gloomy cloud, which more and more looked like a vast net draped over the land. All day, the cloud went on thickening, while the Iron Woman and the Iron Man watched it. In the end, Lucy and Hogarth had to go home beneath it, still hearing that strange sighing groan – which seemed to come from everywhere. They sat for a long time in the bathroom, watching her father's bubbles.

Next morning the house was clear of the gloom. Lucy's father lay with his chin on the bath's edge, waiting to be fed. His bubbling had stopped. And the groaning too, outside, had stopped.

But the sky was dark, as for a heavy thunderstorm. A dense, blue-blackish webby cloud lay very low over everything. The air was still, not a bird moved.

Once again, Lucy and Hogarth climbed through the woods, and came out above the cloud. The two giant figures stood exactly as they had last seen them.

'What's happening?' cried Lucy as they came nearer. 'What's that funny cloud?'

But now they both saw that the eyes of the Iron Woman and the Iron Man were beaming red. Four powerful rays of red light, like laser beams, plunged down into the dark cloud spread out below.

'Something's going on,' whispered Hogarth.

They heard a cry – a sob. It was as loud and vast as the groans of yesterday, but now a sob. And now as Lucy and Hogarth watched they saw a bulge lumping up in the middle of the cloud, over the town. The bulge grew rounder, as if something were pushing an immense head up through it. Then they saw it had eyes. The eyes were so big that it was not really easy to see that they were eyes at all. And there were more than two. But now they had seen them, there was no mistaking them. Vast, mournful eyes. Two huge ones, but then, on either side of them, a slightly smaller one. And two more, slightly smaller again, on either side of those four. Then two more, smaller again. Eight in all. Or was it ten?

And a mouth, a great cloudy cave of gaping mouth, slowly opened, as if it took a long breath. Then came another sob.

The cloud seemed to be one gigantic head, a shapeless, ragged sort of head, like a jellyfish, or like an octopus – spreading out into a vast, knotted tangle of cloudy legs, covering the entire landscape. Or like an immense hairy spider, whose legs spread out across its even more immense web, that lay over the land.

As they watched, the mouth opened wider. The cloud was now sobbing like a giant baby, with wide-open mouth – a mouth that opened wider and wider, squeezing the eyes shut. The four strong red beams from the eyes of the two iron giants plunged into the darkness of the gaping toad-like mouth of the great spider-cloud.

The sobs were now incredibly loud. The spider-face had come closer. It seemed to be resting its chin on the treetops of the wood below. Its row of eyes opened again and gazed woefully down at the two giants, and they heard:

'Release me!'

The words were like the cloud, they filled the whole landscape yet they were blurred, smoky somehow. As if that whole sprawling web were some kind of aerial, transmitting the sounds.

The Iron Woman's voice seemed normal, familiar, in comparison. Yet it was like thunder.

'First,' she said, 'confess who you are.'

The spider-cloud was silent for a while. It seemed surprised. It stared down at the two giants who stared up at it with their crimson beams.

'Confess,' roared the Iron Man, crashing all the gears of his voice.

'Tell us who you are,' thundered the Iron Woman.

The spider-cloud seemed to rear up. Its eyes bulged. Then it bellowed:

'I am the spider-god of Wealth. Wealth. Wealth. The spider-god of more and more and more and more money. I catch it in my web.'

It glared furiously down, and shook the vast web. But the four red laser beams blazed into its eyes and it blinked. It screwed up its eyes and its mouth.

'Now tell us who you really are,' thundered the Iron Woman.

The goblinish cloud snapped its wide, flat mouth. It seemed to bristle and grow even darker. Its eyes crowded close together and sheet lightnings flashed in them.

'I am the spider-god of Gain. The spider-god of winning at all costs. I catch the prize in my net.'

And it reared up to a great height, and let out a tremendous laugh, shaking its web like a cloak the size of the country. The thing that had been groaning so painfully and sobbing so pitifully was laughing.

'Now you've got rid of your lies,' thundered the Iron Woman, 'confess who you really are.'

Both Lucy and Hogarth dropped to the ground. It sounded as though the world had exploded. The vast shape seemed to rear even higher and at the same time to pounce down. To his amazement, Hogarth saw a long bluish tongue flash out of the spider-cloud's mouth, lash around the Iron Man like a whip, and vanish back into the mouth – taking the Iron Man with it.

'Iron Man!' cried Hogarth, as if that could help.

And in that next moment, the long tongue came flashing out again, empty, and whipped itself this time tightly round the Iron Woman.

'Oh no!' screamed Lucy. 'Oh no!'

And sure enough the tongue stopped there – sticking rigidly out full length. It writhed, trying to free itself from the Iron Woman. The cloudy mouth gaped, with squirming lips. The eyes seemed to be climbing down over the great upper lip, to come to the help of the tongue. For the tongue was in trouble. It could not free itself from the Iron Woman. Her fingers were buried in it, like dreadful pincers. The tongue tried to pull itself in through the tightly closed lips, to force her off the end of it. But she was actually climbing up it, hand over hand, dragging the tongue further out between the lips as she clawed her way up.

'Aaaaaagh!' a miserable wail clanged out, echoing off the far corners of the sky. And the spider-cloud reared up, twisting like a whale coming out of the sea, and crashed down on the town. It reared again and crashed again. The mouth gaped, till the eyes popped like blebs on a tyre, as the thing tried to retch. The tongue stuck out, flailing this way and that. Lucy and Hogarth watched aghast. They could see the Iron Woman was now more than halfway up the tongue, climbing slowly towards the tonsils, deep inside the black gape of that mouth, which now stretched so wide it seemed to be trying to turn itself inside out. The sounds of retching were like incessant thunder, as the gigantic dark shape flopped about the landscape. They glimpsed the Iron Woman forcing her way over the root of the tongue into the cavern of the throat. Suddenly the mouth closed and the spider-cloud slumped over the town, silent and motionless.

Lucy and Hogarth stood up. Their faces were white. Their hair stuck out in all directions as if they had been rescued from an explosion. Neither could speak. It really did look as though the Iron Woman and the Iron Man had gone.

But now the cloud was shuddering, and they heard again, just as before, sobbing. Then the Iron Woman's voice, muffled and echoey, came out of the depth of the cloud:

'Confess who you are. Confess. Confess.'

With each word came a thud, that shook the hill under their feet. And at each thud, a strange, gonging boom, like a girder falling inside the hull of a ship. And at each boom, the Cloud-Spider jumped and shook, like a bag with an animal inside it.

'It's the Iron Woman doing her dance,' cried Lucy. 'Inside there. Listen.'

'And that's the Iron Man,' cried Hogarth. 'Beating his chest for a drum, keeping time.'

The Cloud-Spider's lips were opening wide, blubbery and squirming. Big tears squeezed out between the tightly closed eyelids, rolled down, and splashed through on to the town beneath.

'Mess,' wailed the great face. 'Mess.'

'Who are you?' thundered the Iron Woman from deep inside. 'Say it again.' And her pounding dance-steps shook the hill in time to her words, while the Cloud-Spider jerked and contorted, like a rubber comedian's face.

'I am Mess. I am Mess,' came the sobbing wail.

'And who will clean you up?' came the Iron Woman's voice, her words timed to her stamping dance-steps and the weird whanging boom that shook the hill. 'Who will clean you up? Who? Who?'

'Mother,' wailed the vast snail of a mouth.

'Who?'

'Mother.'

'Who?'

'Mother.'

'Tell us again. Who?'

'Mother will clean me up.'

But now the Cloud-Spider was beginning to turn, as the dancing Iron Woman began to turn inside it, dragging it with her like a gown. Its wail grew agonized, higher, thinner. Its edges were being dragged towards that turning centre, like spaghetti being rolled up on a fork. As it turned it rose upwards, turning faster. Soon it was spinning, like an immense whirlpool. The Iron Woman's revolving dance had turned into something else. Something that climbed into a spinning column. The cloudy body and webs of the giant spider were twisted tightly round it.

'It's the Space-Bat-Angel-Dragon,' cried Hogarth. 'Going back up. It's taking the horrible cloud with it.'

'But what about the Iron Woman?' cried Lucy.

Sure enough, the long, swaying, whirling corkscrew of darkness was going up – just as they had seen the

Space-Bat-Angel-Dragon coming down. Lucy and Hogarth couldn't take their eyes off it. The Cloud-Spider was now completely wrapped around that spinning column in tight webby folds, with a few raggy skirts of it flinging out here and there. Somewhere in there the eight eyes must be stretched out long and flat and thin like elastic. But where were the Iron Woman and the Iron Man?

They watched the writhing column climb into the sky, with its corkscrew tip now piercing upwards, worming upwards. Huge and dark and towering, it swayed as it climbed. Growing smaller, as it climbed away. Soon it was a wispy blot, high in the blue. Then a dithering dot, like a skylark. They watched it, and watched it, till at last they were staring into nothing.

They looked down the hill. The air was so clear, in the morning sun, the town seemed to be sparkling. The Iron Woman and the Iron Man were just coming out of the woods, climbing towards them. Lucy ran towards them. Then stopped. Hogarth joined her. The two giants stopped.

'Oh!' cried Lucy. 'Are you all right?' The Iron Woman was no longer a beautiful, gleaming blue-black. She was the colour of an iron fire-grate after many fires, rusty pink and grey-blue. And the Iron Man was the same. As if the inside of the Cloud-Spider had been a furnace of some kind.

'Go home now,' said the Iron Woman. 'And watch. Wait and watch.'

The Iron Man said nothing, just raised his great hand.

Like everybody else, Lucy's mother had heard and watched the tremendous storm of happenings in the dark cloud. And she too had watched the spinning blur climb away into nothing. As if the whole terrific tempest had drained into the blue sky through an upward plughole. She was still standing at the window in a daze when a voice behind her complained:

'Towels, where are all the towels?'

She turned. There was her husband, stark naked except for a skimpy hand towel, shivering and goosepimpled from head to foot, with a seven-day

126

beard, his hair plastered down over his brow, and a woebegone expression on his face. But, worst of all, the stubbly beard and the hair, that should have been black and curly, were now snow white.

'Charlie!' she screamed, and fainted.

So it seemed to be over. All the men climbed out of the rivers, the ponds, the swimming pools, the baths. Women ran everywhere, with bags full of clothes and towels. Slowly, life started up. Lights came on. Cars began to move. Shops opened. Telephones rang incessantly.

But things had changed. For one thing, it was not only Lucy's father whose hair had gone white. Every man who had been a fish, or a seal, or a water-bug, or a leech, now had white hair. Men who had been grizzled, or nearly grey, or grey, stared into their mirrors at their silvery white hair and cried: 'Oh God, I look like Granny!' or else 'But my face isn't any older, is it?' And young men whose hair had been curly gold or glossy auburn brown or mousy hardly dared catch sight of themselves in their car mirror, or in a shop window. 'It's no wonder,' they said to their wives or girlfriends. 'What we went through was no joke. Worse than seeing a thousand ghosts! You'd have gone white too.' Within days, hairdressers and chemists were out of hair dye.

But other things had changed for the better. Everybody realized straightaway that the terrible scream no longer blasted them when they touched each other. Instead they now heard it all the time, but only faintly – like a ringing in the ears. And strangely enough, it came and went.

It was easy to see what made it come. When you looked at the waste bin, it came noticeably stronger. And when you poured soap powder into the washing machine, it seemed to zoom in on you and go past very close, like a jet going over the house – but a jet powered with those screams. It was a bit of a shock. And when Mr Wells, with his little white moustache, looked at his stacked drums of toxic waste, it came nearly full strength, a painful screech in his ears, like something coming straight at him, and he had to look away quickly.

So nobody could forget. Farmers stood in their fields, listening and thinking. Factory owners sat in their offices, listening and thinking. The Prime Minister sat with his Cabinet Ministers, listening and thinking – and whoever spoke, the others looked at the speaker's weirdly white hair and listened more carefully, and thought more deeply.

They had all learned a frightening lesson. But what could they do about it?

They soon found out.

Already, next morning, an odd thing was noticed. The first men back to work at Chicago saw a yellow net, like a massive spider's web, draped thickly over the stacks of drums full of poisonous chemicals. Each strand was the thickness of a pencil, and brittle, so it broke up into short lengths. It was a mystery.

The same webs were draped over all the waste dumps in the country. Over all the rubbish heaps. Over all the lagoons of cattle slurry. The same stuff.

Chemists were baffled by it when they tried to find

out what it was. But pretty soon they found what it was good for. It was the perfect fuel. Dissolved in water, it would do everything that oil and petrol would do, yet fish could live in it. It would burn in a fireplace with a grand flame but no fumes of any kind. And that first morning there were thousands of tons of it.

Next morning, the same. And now everybody could see that the rubbish and the poisonous waste were being mysteriously changed into these yellow webs during the night.

Even if you had a little rubbish heap in your back garden, you would have a web on it next morning. Or a web where it had been. Then you could dissolve it in water and run your car on it for a while.

Strange!

People soon realized what was happening. At nightfall, a mist gathered over any rubbish, wherever it might be. A dark, webby, smoky mist. Just like the clouds of puff that had bubbled from those suffering men when they were fish and newts and frogs. And next morning there was the yellow web – and the rubbish had gone. Or most of it had. Another night and it would be all gone. As if the mist had eaten the rubbish and left a web.

No wonder they called it a miracle. It happened in no other country.

But wherever the rubbish or the waste leaked into a stream or a pond, the mist would not form. Once that leak was stopped, sure enough next night the webs would come. So everybody stopped those leaks because everybody wanted the magic fuel.

Mr Wells didn't have to scratch his bald head for long. He blocked all those outlets into the river and simply stacked the waste – where it soon turned into yellow webs. Then each day his men harvested the yellow webs. Now he could import waste from all over the world. The more the better. All his suppliers had to pay him to take it, of course. Then he sold the yellow webs. Soon he could triple all his wages.

And soon, too, they found it was better than manure. Or, treated this way, it would kill Colorado beetles and nothing else. Treated that way, it would keep out thistles. It could be made to do anything.

Of course, nobody knew what had really happened.

'A miracle!' they said, shaking their heads. 'Truly.'

'Our problems,' said the Prime Minister, 'seem to be strangely solved.'

Hogarth had to go home. On that last morning, he and Lucy climbed the hill together. It was the third day of the webs. Everybody was still baffled by these strange, brittle, yellow nets. Lucy and Hogarth were no wiser than anybody else. But they knew it had to do with that terrific fight, when the Iron Woman had clawed her way down the Cloud-Spider's throat and fought it from the inside with her dreadful dance and the star power of the Space-Bat-Angel-Dragon. Something to do with the way the Space-Bat-Angel-Dragon had whirled it into a spinning blur, and taken it upwards.

There were the Iron Woman and the Iron Man, sitting on the hilltop stones, among the cedars. The Iron Man had brought up the birdwatcher's car out of the marsh. He was folding pieces of it into handy shapes. They seemed to be having a picnic together. Every trace of their scorching and burns had disappeared. In fact they seemed brighter than ever. The Iron Woman's blue-black looked new-made. Lucy wondered if they had been polishing each other. She and Hogarth sat on the grass near by, gazing at them.

'Iron Man, can I ask you something?' said Hogarth after a while.

The Iron Man swivelled his head slightly and stopped chewing, to show he was listening.

'Where are the yellow webs from?' asked Hogarth.

The Iron Man started to chew again. He seemed to be looking at the Iron Woman. Minutes passed. Finally the Iron Woman spoke.

'Where from?' she said. And paused.

She went on chewing a while. She was bent over something in her lap, that she worked at carefully. Then her voice came again, rumbling somehow from beneath them, or echoing somehow from all around them. 'Where,' she asked, 'did the Cloud-Spider come from?'

'The bubbles!' cried Lucy. How could she forget those bubbles.

The Iron Woman chewed. She seemed not to have heard, as she worked at whatever it was in her lap. Then her voice came again: 'And the bubbles? Where did they come from?'

Both Lucy and Hogarth were thinking the same thing. Obviously the bubbles had come from – well, from inside Lucy's father, for one. When he was a giant newt. And from inside Hogarth's father when he was a giant frog. And from inside all the other men.

Lucy frowned. Was the Iron Woman saying that the yellow webs, or whatever was making the yellow webs, was the same thing that made the bubbles? Inside her father? And inside the others? Somehow? How could that be? But the Iron Woman's voice was rumbling again.

'Big, deep fright,' she said. 'Big, deep change.'

Lucy thought about her father's hair. That was big change, all right. But still, it was only hair. Whatever had made those bubbles – that's where the change must be. That was deep. But what was it? And how could it . . .? Lucy and Hogarth were lost in their thoughts, as they gazed up at the huge, mysterious faces.

Then the Iron Woman reached out and laid over Lucy's shoulders a heavy, cool necklace made of flowers from every month in the year. Later, when Lucy counted them, there were fifty-two different kinds of flowers. The giant hands came out again and laid another flower necklace, exactly the same, over Hogarth's shoulders. Then she lifted both her hands and laid another flower necklace, very much bigger, very thick and heavy, made entirely of foxgloves, round the neck of the Iron Man. Finally, she put one over her own head, and arranged it across her breast. This one, Lucy saw, was made entirely of snowdrops.

The four of them sat there, in the warm, morning sun, not saying anything. Lucy and Hogarth simply watched the huge faces of their strange friends, and listened to the faint sound in their ears. This sound, they now noticed, seemed to have become stronger and different. It was not the faint sound of the creatures crying. It was music of a kind, from far off, far up. They both looked up into the blue, gazing and listening. It was not a skylark.